ALSO BY MAXINE CHERNOFF

FICTION

PLAIN GRIEF

BOP

POETRY

LEAP YEAR DAY: NEW AND SELECTED POEMS

NEW FACES OF 1952

JAPAN

UTOPIA TV STORE

■ ■ ■ ■ ■ ■ ■ ■ ■ ■ ■ ■ ■ ■ ■ ■ ■

MAXINE CHERNOFF

SIGNS OF DEVOTION

STORIES

SIMON & SCHUSTER
NEW YORK LONDON TORONTO SYDNEY TOKYO SINGAPORE

SIMON & SCHUSTER
SIMON & SCHUSTER BUILDING
ROCKEFELLER CENTER
1230 AVENUE OF THE AMERICAS
NEW YORK, NEW YORK 10020

THIS BOOK IS A WORK OF FICTION. NAMES, CHARACTERS, PLACES AND INCIDENTS ARE EITHER PRODUCTS OF THE AUTHOR'S IMAGINATION OR ARE USED FICTITIOUSLY. ANY RESEMBLANCE TO ACTUAL EVENTS OR LOCALES OR PERSONS, LIVING OR DEAD, IS ENTIRELY COINCIDENTAL.

COPYRIGHT © 1993 BY MAXINE CHERNOFF

ALL RIGHTS RESERVED
INCLUDING THE RIGHT OF REPRODUCTION
IN WHOLE OR IN PART IN ANY FORM.

SIMON AND SCHUSTER AND COLOPHON ARE REGISTERED TRADEMARKS OF SIMON & SCHUSTER INC.

DESIGNED BY SONGHEE KIM

MANUFACTURED IN THE UNITED STATES OF AMERICA

1 3 5 7 9 10 8 6 4 2

LIBRARY OF CONGRESS CATALOGING-IN-PUBLICATION DATA
CHERNOFF, MAXINE, DATE.
SIGNS OF DEVOTION: STORIES / MAXINE CHERNOFF.
I. TITLE.
PS3553.H356S58   1993
813' .54—DC20   92-47368
CIP
ISBN 0-671-79812-X

In "Baudelaire's Drainpipe" a slightly altered line from the poem "Soft Letter" by Peter Schjeldahl, from the collection *White Country*, appears with the author's permission.

FOR KOREN, JULIAN, PHILIP,
AND ALWAYS FOR PAUL

ACKNOWLEDGMENTS

■ ■ ■ ■ ■ ■ ■ ■ ■ Some of these stories, in slightly different form, have been published in the following magazines and anthologies. My thanks to their editors.

Thanks as well to Rebecca Saletan at Simon & Schuster and to Amanda Urban.

"Signs of Devotion" in *The Marriage Bed* (HarperCollins)
"Baudelaire's Drainpipe" in *Ploughshares*
"Death Swap" in *Mississippi Review*
"The Stockholm Syndrome" in *Story*
"Element 109" in *Mississippi Review*
"Keys" in *Formations*
"Somewhere Near Tucson" in *North American Review*
"Something to Admire" in *Santa Monica Review*
"Jury Duty" in *St. Mark's Papers*, *ACM*, and *Woman's Glib* (Crossing Press)
"The River Shannon" in *Caprice*
"Saving the Australian Elephant" in *New American Writing*
"Kabuki Everything" in *ACM*
"California" in *West Side Stories* (City Stoop Press) and *B-City*
"As Sure as Albert Schweitzer" in *ACM*
"Six-Oh" in *Painted Bride Quarterly*
"The Untouchables" in *New Chicago Stories* (City Stoop Press)
"Heathcliff" in *What!* and *Emergence*

CONTENTS

■ ■ ■ ■ ■ ■ ■ ■ ■ ■ ■ ■ ■

JURY DUTY ■ **11**

BAUDELAIRE'S DRAINPIPE ■ **15**

THE UNTOUCHABLES ■ **23**

DEATH SWAP ■ **35**

HEATHCLIFF ■ **47**

THE STOCKHOLM SYNDROME ■ **57**

SAVING THE AUSTRALIAN ELEPHANT ■ **67**

KEYS ■ **75**

ELEMENT 109 ■ **83**

SIGNS OF DEVOTION ■ **91**

THE RIVER SHANNON ■ **101**

SIX-OH ■ **109**

SOMEWHERE NEAR TUCSON ■ **125**

WHERE EVENTS MAY LEAD ■ **135**

KABUKI EVERYTHING ■ **149**

CALIFORNIA ■ **163**

SOMETHING TO ADMIRE ■ **181**

NOVEMBER ■ **193**

TWO MEN ■ **205**

AS SURE AS ALBERT SCHWEITZER ■ **215**

SIGNS OF DEVOTION

JURY DUTY

■ ■ ■ ■ ■ ■ ■ ■ ■ I had spent the first part of the summer distraught, writing a story about a woman I know, a lesbian, who had a baby. I wanted to do the story justice, nothing preachy or high-toned, just honest observation and discussion. The story was boring. It was boring to me when I was writing it, and I assumed it would be boring to anyone who might read it. Brenda and Mary were portrayed as loving, concerned future parents, the problems of pregnancy discussed with sympathy. Integrity was my byword. In my story Brenda was fertilized at a medical center by a doctor she called The Inseminator. The best scene involved the couple's sitting at the breakfast table, sharing a muffin, telling insemination jokes. They weren't male stand-up comic jokes that someone like Tom Dreessen might tell, but a scenario involving a series of movies called *The Inseminator*. Arnold Schwarzenegger would fertilize whole cities, metropoli, continents. This was the comic relief. In art, as in life, accidents happen, and Brenda lost her baby. I kept hoping as I wrote the story that I wasn't punishing her by resolving the plot in that way. I went through the list of all my friends who'd miscarried and felt reassured that at least in real life justice plays no role.

Then two things happened. First, my good friend Lois told me that the woman on whom I'd based Brenda had fallen in love with the man who'd gotten her pregnant. In

JURY DUTY

real life Brenda hadn't gone to a doctor at all. She'd gone to the Drake Hotel, and when her basal temperature was perfectly adjusted, had made love to her friend's friend Mark, a book designer. She's the kind of person who cuts corners. Her night of heterosexual passion led to Kyle, who's now almost two, and is said to resemble Mark more strongly than Brenda. Meanwhile, Mark had begun to call. It was only natural that he'd be interested in his son. They had dinner a few times and one thing led to another. Now Brenda's wearing makeup again, seeing Mark regularly, and having very little to do with Mary, the woman with whom she was supposed to be raising Kyle.

Lois spared no details. The makeup she can accept. After all, who doesn't want to look nice? Why should women deny themselves what's best from the past to make a statement about the present that's finally puritanical? "No, the makeup is great," Lois said. "Besides, even men wear makeup these days. My butcher wears something that keeps his skin looking tight and young. It's the damned shoes."

"The shoes?"

"She buys shoes to match all her outfits now. She's a regular Imelda. And the hair. It's sleek. It's contemporary. It could co-anchor the news without a face to hold it up."

"Good for her," I said, thinking that my story was probably too weighty and moralistic. "As long as she's happy."

"Good for Kyle that the father's interested. Old Brenda's too ditzy to raise that child herself."

"So it's a happy ending?"

"Not really. It's a crying shame. Why is it love that always changes women? Even in the highest art. Even in Jane Austen. Why can't it be nautical adventure or politics or ideas?"

SIGNS OF DEVOTION

I was thinking this over Monday morning when I arrived for jury duty. It was the Criminal Court, where I hoped I might get involved in a short, interesting case that would yield a story. Twelve weeks on Claus Von Bulow didn't appeal to my immediate sense of my future self. I had stories to write, dinners to cook, a tennis backhand to improve. Give me a small murder, an unambiguous kidnapping. Give me a purse thief with musical abilities or a man who's pruned his neighbor's tree while high on angel dust. Let me be out of here by rush hour.

I spent nearly the entire week of jury duty sitting on the bench. Twice I was asked not to read. Many potential jurors snored blissfully around me. None was asked not to sleep. The third time I began reading nobody bothered me. I was set in my ways. Besides, the book was nonfiction. I was a serious person. The book's cover was navy blue. The title was engraved.

While sitting on the bench waiting to be called, I spent part of each day staring at a pregnant woman. She was small and dark, maybe Indian or Pakistani, and sweated profusely. I wondered if she really had to endure the week or could have used her pregnancy as an excuse. I wondered if she would have liked my story about Brenda. I began thinking of pregnancy itself as a form of jury duty. I remembered when I had my first child. The nurse held her up to my face, but because I wasn't wearing glasses and was groggy from labor, I thought the nurse's elbow was part of my daughter's back, a protrusion.

"She's beautiful," they assured me, but I was overcome by fear and unable to ask about what I suspected until a second viewing.

JURY DUTY

At the time of my jury duty, I was on a medication for my nerves. I'd been having panic attacks in unlikely places. One, for instance, had been in a women's locker room at a YMCA. Its origin remained a mystery. The others—before lecturing to my class on deconstruction, while driving to work, visiting my mother at the hospital—I could explain. Not understanding my latest one sent me straight to my physician.

"Can you help me?" was all I wanted to know.

Before he answered, he made his eyes small and meaningful and told me all about his own panic, panic while giving a medical paper on liver disease, panic at his father's funeral.

"Did your father have liver disease?"

"A boating accident," he replied, and wrote me a prescription for a new drug that nips panic in the bud. No more adrenaline coursing through my system like a commuter train to Tokyo. It was his simile, and I thanked him.

The trial on which I actually served as an alternate involved a gang shooting in February. I mention the month because crimes of passion seem barely plausible in winter. A bloodless killer, I concluded, a sociopath. Even before the gun with his fingerprints had been introduced and the witnesses had given their testimony, my mind was made up. I'd rewrite the story. Mary would kill Brenda for having betrayed her. It was plausible. It was justice. It would happen in August.

BAUDELAIRE'S DRAINPIPE

On the last day of our vacation in Paris, I was thinking that it's better to be content at Our Lady of Perpetual Aluminum Siding than to feel disappointment at Notre Dame Cathedral. John, sitting beside me during the Spanish-language service, held my hand and stared down at the floor. He looked morose because the day had already failed to contribute the poignancy he demanded of our travels. I whispered to him that missing a tour of Baudelaire's house was nothing to pout about, but John was inconsolable.

I wondered if some people are naturally drawn to beauty, others to necessity. My sister has a son who pointed his baby hand, declaring objects beautiful as soon as he could speak. My aesthetic ledger contains many blank pages and is opened only under special circumstances. Its entries are for what I imagine beauty might be at a distance. On my bedroom wall as a child I had a travel poster of Portofino. My mother had placed it there because the glistening water and sandy winding path blended with my draperies. Her decorating concept was my touchstone for beauty. Finding myself in Portofino twenty years later, I was more aware of the shooting pain in my Achilles tendon and the tingle of my skin as the sun pierced the back of my polo shirt. As hymns were sung and the collection plate was passed, I reduced my philosophy to a slogan: It's better to have seen Baudelaire's

BAUDELAIRE'S DRAINPIPE

drainpipe than to have missed the house altogether.

Besides, some aesthetic notions can be dangerous. I read in the paper back home that a neighborhood teenager wanted to change his image by giving himself a Mohawk. He asked his grandmother for an electric razor. When she was unable to find it, he stalked her around the house with a baseball bat, a Raskolnikov of New Wave. The story was printed in the local crime blotter, but it seems more a cautionary tale about ardor. Until I read that story, I hadn't thought much about a line in a poem that said, "Too much beauty could detonate us." Looking at John moping next to me, I wondered if too little beauty could produce the same effect.

John had a profound reaction to Baudelaire's house being around the corner from our hotel yet inaccessible. He stormed around the bird market banging into cages, swearing under his breath. I suggested we visit Notre Dame again, hoping its grimacing angels might offer commiseration. As we walked there, he recounted all the places we hadn't seen in our travels. It was a list of startling variety, with nuances of hope, resolve, and despair. It contained a Buddhist temple we were unable to locate on a remote mountain in Japan; the shrine at Delos, unapproachable by boat in rough water; London's Highgate Cemetery, padlocked to visitors; Freud's house in Vienna, closed for remodeling. Later at a café he actually wrote out the list after ordering a second espresso. Before I could remind him that we had been successful on other occasions, a goat had climbed a ladder set up on the sidewalk and his trainer was extending a red metal coin box in our direction. The goat

SIGNS OF DEVOTION

wore a green Alpine hat and made me recall an out-of-context camel we'd chosen not to mount for a photo years ago on Crete.

I reminded John that we'd seen many sights. My list ranged from Apollinaire's grave to locks of Keats's hair to the birth of our own daughter. I thought I might jostle him into better cheer by adding that final intimate detail, but John was unwilling to be consoled. His list continued. It included the Pope at Yankee Stadium and Simon and Garfunkel in Central Park. When I told him that he didn't even like Simon and Garfunkel, he said that was beside the point. I looked at his troubled eyes and wondered why he took these disappointments personally. Someday, I worried, he might read a news story about trash dumped in space, say, "Look what they've done to my galaxy!" and jump out a window.

Now the street performer tied the goat to the ladder and took a little dog dressed like a clown out of a carrying case. The man was dressed in black tights that made his legs seem spindly. The dog looked perilously mortal. It was an aged chihuahua, categorically uninterested in the commands that the man delivered in increasingly loud, vehement French. I suggested to John that right now we were witnessing something memorable, France's most inept dog trainer. Usually he would have laughed at that, but instead he described Baudelaire's drainpipe in detail, as if he were fixing it in his mind.

"Bronze," he said. "A fish whose head points downward and whose tail is soldered to the drainpipe itself."

"I'm not sure," I answered, "that the fish is turned upside

BAUDELAIRE'S DRAINPIPE

down. Maybe the fish's mouth is open, and the drainpipe emerges from it. I think I remember the tail curled in one direction or another at the bottom."

He turned his face away from me and watched the man throw small embroidery hoops over the dog's neck. Then the man picked up the dog and tossed him onto the goat's back. The dog's hind legs quivered with tension.

"We'll have to go and look at it again." John slugged down his espresso and started off in the direction of Baudelaire's corner. I followed him silently down the narrow lanes of L'Île St. Louis. When we approached the entrance to our hotel, I told him I was going to take a nap. He looked at me wearily and said he'd take a picture of the drainpipe, since I wasn't interested enough to join him.

I must have slept for a long time. I woke up in darkness and thought about a museum in Montreal where we'd seen an exhibit of Rodchenko's Futurist furniture, an aesthetic based on perceptual miscues. Chairs that resembled greyhounds seemed too fragile to sit on. I remembered a museum for children with a room that distorted perspective and how happily my nephew, the one who loved beauty, had sashayed up and down the slanting floor.

When John finally returned, he didn't say a word. He'd brought a sack filled with dinner items that he noisily unwrapped. He placed a tin of sardines next to a ball of cheese. Then he unwrapped a pentagon-shaped slab of bread. Next to it he placed two orange-yellow pears, a bottle of Bordeaux with a swan on the label, and some chocolates with hazelnuts from Italy. Someone should have painted it all before I bit into a slightly unripe pear.

"Did you see Baudelaire's drainpipe?" I asked him.

"Remember that bus ride in the Philippines?" he asked.

That called me back to our days in the Peace Corps before Glenna was born. I wasn't sure which bus ride he had in mind, though most were of the same character and duration: stifling, acrid, and endless. "Which exact one?" I finally asked, tearing a corner of crusty bread from the loaf.

"The one with the chickens and pigs and the man who bumped his head on the roof of the bus when we went over a rut in the road."

"Not really," I said.

"The man's head bled, and the people on the bus pointed and laughed. You were irate. You don't remember that?"

"It all sounds familiar, but I can't say that I actually remember."

"Then my afternoon's been a waste," he said, shrugging his shoulders. He speared a sardine with surprising ferocity. "Why do I need to take photos when I can tell you anything, and you'll believe me?"

When we got back to New York a week later, the photos we'd taken in Paris were developed. There was Père Lachaise Cemetery with Apollinaire's flower-strewn grave. There was our tour guide, whose radiant copper-colored eyes shone like new pennies. There I was, smiling in the bird market on that ill-fated Sunday. Among the photos I saw no evidence of Baudelaire's drainpipe, but I decided not to reopen the case.

A few weeks later we were dining with Glenna and Ramon. It's hard to believe that my daughter's a married

BAUDELAIRE'S DRAINPIPE

woman with a baby of her own. John was holding little Aaron and playing with his fingers when Glenna asked him how we'd liked Paris. John said I'd been satisfied enough, having lower standards than he does. Glenna wondered whether the hotel wasn't up to par.

Preparing to respond, he handed back the baby, and I said, "Dad means Baudelaire's home. We missed the weekly tour by fifteen minutes. We did see his drainpipe, though, and it was lovely."

John snorted with disdain. I wondered how I could love this man.

To make matters worse, Glenna started laughing. "Remember Melville's toolshed and Emily Dickinson's parking meter? Didn't we drive two hundred miles to see them?"

"Quiet, you'll wake the baby," John told Glenna.

"The baby's awake," Glenna said, coaxing Aaron's head under her blouse to nurse him.

John turned away from Glenna and me, adjusted his glasses and spoke. "Women don't understand the purpose of traveling," John told Ramon in a confidential whisper.

"Who was Baudelaire?" Ramon asked.

I was just brushing my teeth before bed when John flashed a photo in front of my eyes. He moved it into and out of my field of vision so quickly that I wasn't sure what I'd seen. "What was that?" I asked him.

"Baudelaire's drainpipe," he answered, voice registering triumph.

"Then you were right about the fish?" I asked him.

"No," he said smugly, "but at least I cared enough to do the necessary research."

SIGNS OF DEVOTION

• • •

The next morning John told me that he was sick of traveling. He thought it would be better for us to stay home in the future. He pointed at an island-shaped place on the kitchen ceiling where the plaster needed repair. He gestured outside to our crumbling staircase veined with weeds and fledgling trees.

I looked up from the garden catalog I'd been reading. "Look," I said pointing. "Green tulips. Don't they remind you of something?" John kissed me on my shoulder and said no. I was thinking of the color of old bronze, the color the drainpipe fish had become over a century of weather and change.

■ ■ ■ ■ ■ ■ ■ ■ ■ ■ ■ ■ ■ ■ ■ ■ ■

THE UNTOUCHABLES

■ ■ ■ ■ ■ ■ ■ ■ ■ Jane knew that her father, a leather-goods salesman, was of the merchant class. She had been studying the caste system in school and worried that his job might put him in jeopardy, since Untouchables dealt with animal skins. As long as her father only sold the stuff, he'd be safe. Salespeople were never Untouchables. She would have liked her father to have been a Brahmin, but after all, her family lived next to a gas station and showed no particular interest in learning or religion. Usually this pleased her. While her Catholic friends were tortured in Sunday clothes, Jane could ride around the block on her old Schwinn bike singing "Some Enchanted Evening," her favorite song from *South Pacific*. Every time she passed the Shell station, she'd ride over the hose that made the bell ring. Sometimes it punctuated the song mid-chorus. Other times it accompanied her as she reached for a high note. When she got bored, she'd park her bike, walk back to the gas station, put her quarter in for a Coke and swig the bottle down leaning against the red metal housing of the machine. No one noticed her. She could stare at anyone she pleased. Mostly she looked at the *m'woman*, which was what her father called the person who pumped gas on weekends.

Jane had concluded that the m'woman was definitely a woman because the badge on her shirt didn't lie flat over her breast pocket. It puckered, as her own pockets had begun to. But no woman in her right mind would have shaved her hair way above the ear or that short on the neck and let grease accumulate all over her face and hands without trying to clean herself up. Once Jane asked her mother about the m'woman but was told to be quiet. If she'd followed with "Why?" one of her parents would have said, "'Why' is a Chinaman's name," which had never made any sense to her. Victoria Pranz's mother had told Jane that the m'woman was probably a lesbian. Victoria's mother was definitely a Brahmin, an art professor at the University of Chicago, though her status was questionable, considering her recent divorce.

Dr. Pranz would be a Brahmin too, Jane calculated, by virtue of his classical music training. Even though he'd given up the flute to practice dentistry, he might have played in a symphony. Once Victoria had told Jane that dentists have the highest suicide rates. From then on Jane had stared at Dr. Pranz, trying to detect a sudden sadness behind his jocular manner and jaunty little Vandyke. When he left Mrs. Pranz, Jane wondered if he'd take to wandering aimlessly along Lake Michigan until a surge of emotions vaulted him into the water. But when he came to pick up Victoria on Saturdays, he never looked anything but animated. Sometimes he'd include Jane in a special outing. En route he'd hum to the classical music on the car radio. One morning they'd gone to Calumet Harbor to tour a merchant-marine ship from Denmark. Someone depressed couldn't have thought of such pastimes. Jane's own father, absorbed in the Cubs' problems with left-handed hitting, or bills or edging the lawn, looked far sadder than Dr. Pranz.

Perhaps Brahmins were naturally more content than the merchant class.

On Sundays Victoria and Jane rode their bikes together. On the particular Sunday it happened, Jane was in the lead, Victoria well behind. That was a difference between them. Victoria dallied, taking in details, reserving judgment. Maybe she'd inherited her mother's preoccupation with seeing. Jane remembered a horrible Columbus Day spent at the Art Institute with Victoria and her mother, who paused for one, sometimes two minutes, at every painting before moving on. Even worse, Mrs. Pranz asked Jane what she thought of several Cézannes, as if Jane could tell her something she didn't already know. "You're the artist," Jane had finally said when Mrs. Pranz seemed dissatisfied with her replying, "I think they're okay."

When Jane went over the gas hose this time, her tire skidded in some grease and she went flying over the handlebars, landing on both palms and knees. Before Victoria caught up with her, the m'woman had rushed out of the gas station and was helping Jane up. She made a greasy fist around Jane's forearm. Pulling Jane to her feet, she surveyed the damage. "Guess you'll be all right," she said and offered Jane a clean flannel cloth. Jane stared at her palms, which were red and smarting under the grease, and at her poor knees, which had taken the brunt of the fall. One was bloodier than the other. Jane dabbed at them with the rag. Before Victoria arrived on the scene, the m'woman had walked back into the garage.

"She talked to me!" Jane told Victoria as they walked their bikes home.

"Who?" Victoria asked, cocking her head like her mother while waiting for the reply.

"The m'woman came out when I fell. She has a lady's voice. She gave me this cloth." Jane held it out.

"Yuck," Victoria said.

By then they'd reached Jane's house. As Jane expected, her mother asked Victoria to go home. Whenever Jane got hurt, her mother used the occasion to lecture not only about safety but whatever had been on her mind since the last injury.

"Let's go to Woolworth's," her mother said, wiping the last grease off Jane's legs. "I need some yarn, and I'll buy you a vanilla Coke."

Bandages on both palms and knees, Jane limped to the Fairlane. She made a halfhearted effort to comb her hair and wet her lips shiny as her mother started the car and headed off.

"Jane, I was wondering, honey, whether I've told you enough."

"About what?" Jane asked, alert to a very different line of questioning.

"About growing up," her mother said.

"I guess it's just happening anyway," Jane said, looking down at her hands, which, with the extra bandages and the stiffness they caused, appeared huge.

"I mean something else," her mother mumbled. Why wasn't Mrs. Pranz her mother? She had brought home a gynecological text and taken Victoria to a health seminar on her eleventh birthday. Whenever Jane's mother wanted to talk about sex, she got all self-conscious and stuttery and even drove funny.

SIGNS OF DEVOTION

"Mom, you're going twelve miles an hour. I think the speed's at least twenty-five."

"Do you know about babies?" Jane's mother blurted out as she parallel-parked the car in front of Woolworth's. Parking had taken three tries.

"They're those little things with diapers, right, Mom?"

Before her mother could reply, their attention was caught by the couple standing in front of Woolworth's. The thin young man had his arms around the girl, who was younger still, perhaps sixteen. Her hands were tucked demurely in her pockets. What fascinated Jane was how their bodies connected at the tongue, and how they twisted against each other for what seemed like forever.

"They're Frenching," Jane explained to her mother, who looked either confused or stricken. "Hey, that's Nina Treesom!" she added. Nina lived across the alley and had been dating a college boy.

"Hi, Nina," Jane said, as her mother whisked her past them into the store.

"Yarn?" her mother asked, a tired monosyllable. The woman pointed them toward the back of the store, Jane's favorite area, where she could watch the parakeets crowding together, chirping on their perches.

Her mother bought pink and blue and yellow mohair, promising Jane she'd make her a sweater. Every so often she took on such projects, but most ended in failure. There was a whole box of half-made sweaters and scarves in the bottom of the linen closet. Jane said that would be nice, but spent her time over the vanilla Coke thinking about the m'woman. After the flannel cloth was clean, Jane would return it to her. Maybe the m'woman would explain to her

■ 27

why she dressed that way. Maybe she was from another country, but Jane hadn't detected an accent.

"The couple you saw outside Woolworth's," her mother began once she was back behind the wheel, "had better be careful." She was shaking a manicured index finger toward Jane's nose.

"Mom, that was Nina. Remember, she used to walk me to school when I was in kindergarten?"

"Nina or not, one thing leads to another." Squinting to look serious, she added, "Remember Tammy Swartz?"

"Yes," Jane said, recalling Mrs. Swartz's hefty daughter who'd gone away one summer to work at a resort in the Wisconsin Dells.

"She didn't go to college after that summer, Jane, like Mrs. Swartz told everyone. She had a baby."

"But she wasn't married."

"I'm telling you, Jane, it's dangerous to be a woman." She was looking crazed again. They took a sharp left. The tires squealed around their corner, engraving the afternoon on Jane's eardrums, and they were home.

Jane lay on her bed and wondered whether the m'woman worried about such matters. It would be nice to worry about nothing at all or just dumb things like her father did. Jane wondered what the m'woman's status would be in India. Then she remembered that unmarried women were always a disgrace to their families.

When Jane walked into the gas-station garage, the m'woman was reading the Sunday paper and smoking a cigarette. She had stretched out her legs so that her work boots rested against the edge of the counter.

SIGNS OF DEVOTION

"Excuse me," Jane said.

The m'woman looked up and smiled at her.

"I have your cloth." Jane held it toward her.

"Thanks," the m'woman said. "Are you all healed?"

"I'm fine," Jane said. She noticed that the insignia over the m'woman's pocket read "Ike." She smiled to think that the m'woman and the President shared the same name.

"I'm Jane."

"I'm Sheila."

"Your pocket says 'Ike.'"

"I'm Sheila Ikenberry. People call me Ike."

"I'm twelve."

"I'm thirty-two."

Then the gas-bell rang, and a blue Chevy was waiting at a pump.

"Right back," Ike said.

Jane picked up the paper Ike had been reading. It was folded at the classified-car ads.

"I'm looking for a car," Ike said.

"My dad buys Fords."

"Right now I have a Studebaker." She pointed outside to a two-toned sedan colored like toast with jelly. "It's getting kind of old, and I live way out in the sticks. I need a more dependable car for winter."

"My mom drives my dad's car. Someday I'll probably have my own car. I wouldn't mind a Thunderbird."

"Right now your bike is fine, I'd guess."

"Sure it is. I'm talking about the future."

"What do you want to be in the future?" Ike asked.

This is leading somewhere, Jane thought. If she just said the right thing, Ike would explain herself. "Maybe a truck driver," Jane said, hoping to prod her along.

"When I was little, I wanted to be a nurse."

A Plymouth pulled up. The man got out of the car and walked into the gas station.

"Got some change for the Coke machine?" he asked. Ike gave him quarters, nickles, and dimes.

"Your hair's pretty short," Jane said while the man was opening his Coke.

"Yeah, it's convenient for me that way." Ike picked up her paper and started looking down the column again. "I used to wear it longer when I was your age." She drew red circles around two car ads in a row.

"Do you have any pictures?" Jane asked.

"Of what?"

"Your family, or how you looked before you cut your hair."

"Not on me," Ike said. "Why don't you come by next Sunday? I'll bring a photo of me when I was your age."

"I'll try," said Jane. "Mostly I'm free on Sundays."

"Want a Coke?"

"I don't have any money."

"I'll treat you to one," Ike said, "and then I have to close up for the day."

All the time Jane drank the Coke, she watched Ike reading the ads. Ike never looked up or seemed to notice that Jane was staring. If she did notice, she ignored it, just as she did Jane's riding over the gas-station hose again and again.

That Tuesday Mrs. Pranz took Jane and Victoria back to the Art Institute. In one gallery right near *American Gothic,* which Jane remembered from her previous visit, she saw a painting she hadn't noticed before. It was a gas station painted at night by someone named Edward Hopper. The station itself was lit up and the majestic red pumps were topped off with white globes. There was a lone attendant standing at one edge of the painting and a road that went off into darkness. Jane liked how the painting admitted that gas stations mattered. She hoped Mrs. Pranz would ask her about it. For once she'd have had something to say.

On the way out Mrs. Pranz asked the girls what they'd like in the gift shop. Victoria picked out some stationery with Degas dancers. Jane chose a few postcards. Between a Renoir mother and child and Van Gogh's bedroom, Jane slipped the Hopper painting.

Because it was raining that Sunday, it was harder for Jane to get out of the house. She knew she couldn't just say she was going to the gas station or mention Ike's name, even as Sheila Ikenberry. She was glad for one thing. Her mother had gotten all involved in the sweater and forgotten about Jane's education in being a woman.

"I'm taking a bike ride," Jane said. Her father, who was reading *National Geographic*, didn't look up.

"In the rain?" her mother asked, peering over her glasses.

"I need a few things at Woolworth's," Jane said, "and I want to look at the parakeets."

"Don't look too long," her father said, "or they'll charge you."

Ike was sitting exactly where she'd been last week. She was wearing a rubber raincoat over her slacks and shirt.

"Lousy weather to pump gas," she said when Jane walked in. "On days like this I wish I *had* been a nurse."

"I guess you still could be," Jane said but regretted it im-

THE UNTOUCHABLES

mediately. It was the kind of thing her mother would have said to cheer someone up.

Ike smiled and opened the drawer under the cash register. "Voilà!" She produced a picture of herself as a little girl. "That's me at six. I couldn't find me at twelve. Pretty cute, huh?"

She was sitting on a stuffed bear at a zoo. Her hair was short and the little skirt she wore revealed thick, sturdy legs. Because she was smiling into the sun, her face was wrinkled up.

"Where was it taken?" Jane asked.

"The Bronx Zoo. That's where I grew up. Not in the zoo. In the Bronx." She laughed.

"Why did you come to Chicago?"

"Just to follow a friend. The friend was going to move here, so I did too."

"Where's your friend now?"

"That's a long story." Ike looked out the window.

"I brought you something," Jane said, reaching under her rain slicker and pulling out the postcard. She placed it on the counter next to the cash register.

"A postcard of a gas station," Ike said. "Now when I'm at home, I'll be able to remember where I work on weekends." She laughed. "It's really very nice, especially those old-fashioned pumps."

"It's of a painting at the Art Institute."

"Right. A pretty nice painting."

"I go there all the time with Victoria and her mom. Her mom's an art professor."

"I saw you yesterday with your mom. Pardon me for saying this, but your mom's driving leaves something to be desired."

SIGNS OF DEVOTION

"She just learned two years ago. Believe me, she's gotten better. Did your mom drive?"

"My mom didn't drive and neither did my dad. My older brother drove, though. He taught me one summer."

"Why didn't they drive?" Jane asked.

"You ask a lot of questions," Ike said. "How about a little break? Can I buy you another Coke?"

They were at the machine when Jane saw her father approaching. He was wearing a rubber raincoat identical to Ike's.

"Jane, I saw your bike. You're wanted at home," he said.

"Dad, this is Sheila Ikenberry."

"Pleased to meet you," he said, turning to hold the door for Jane.

"Do you spend a lot of time there?" he asked when they were out of the rain under the overhanging porch of their house.

"Not really," Jane said. "Ike saw when I fell off my bike. She came out and asked if I was all right. I guess that got us talking."

"You know, Jane, there's something strange about that woman."

"Daddy, you call her 'the m'woman.' Anyone can see there's something strange about her."

"You probably shouldn't hang around there. Let's not tell Mom for now. She's off in all directions with worries."

"Yeah, what's her problem?"

"Well, we didn't tell you, but for a while we thought that she might be having another baby. Then we found out that she wasn't."

"Is that why she needed yarn?" Jane asked.

"No, she needed yarn later. After she found out she wasn't going to have another baby."

"Why would you want another baby," Jane asked, "when you have me?" For a reason she didn't understand, she felt tears forming in her eyes. She knew her eyes turned greener when she cried. She didn't know if she was crying because she wanted her parents all to herself or didn't want them at all.

They were standing in the foyer when her mother asked where Jane had been. Her father held his finger up to his lips, looked Jane in the eye, and said, "Oh, just around the neighborhood. I treated her to a Coke at the Shell."

The next Sunday Jane looked up Martinegro's Shell Station in the phone book. When Sheila Ikenberry answered, Jane said she thought she'd just say hello. Then she told Ike that her mother had been pregnant but that things hadn't worked out.

"I mailed that postcard to my friend," Ike said. "You know, the one of the gas station? I thought she'd get a kick out of seeing what I've made of myself."

DEATH SWAP

"Is Lou Reed Jewish?" Frank asks Della.

"How do I know? Do you think we're all acquainted with each other?" Della wipes sweat off her eyebrows, which are heavy and slightly curly. No one else is at the pool, which looks like a blue lima bean. She peers toward the dining-room door, hoping that someone will step through it. Not that she's seen anyone interesting or young at the Napa Glen Lodge. The rest of the guests resemble her grandparents. She wonders if young people go on vacation these days.

"I'm just reading this article, and Lou Reed says he admires Bob Dylan and Paul Simon." Frank swats a place on his back where a fly has landed, then cries out in pain. He shouldn't have gotten so much sun. Looking at his legs, which are striped pink, he imagines them as landing strips in a jungle recently cleared by natives.

"My mother called," Della says.

"If a man bites a dog, that's news," Frank answers, letting the magazine fall over his forehead. He turns on his side, extending his knees toward Della. He performs this act slowly, since his back is so tender. Lying this way, he can admire Della as something composed of tan flesh, muscular shoulders, firm breasts and long legs. For a minute he feels content again, as if their vacation isn't an acknowledged mistake they have to endure for three more days.

DEATH SWAP

"Mom hasn't called since we were back home. I don't know why it pisses you off that she calls."

Frank watches Della wait for his response. Her upper lip is squeezed together like a piece of soft candy.

"Why did she name you Della? It's old-fashioned."

"That's the point. After Della Street."

"What?"

"The woman on the 'Perry Mason' show. Oh, I forgot. You only watch Madonna on MTV. You wouldn't know who Perry Mason is."

"He's the guy in the wheelchair who solves crimes even though he's grossly overweight."

"Fact check. That's Ironside, a later incarnation of Raymond Burr. At least you have the right actor." Della closes her eyes and hums something to herself.

Frank thinks of Della singing "Like a Virgin." In his mental video, her body looks even more desirable, legs dangling from Madonna's black garter belt. If she'd only have fewer opinions they'd get along fine, Frank thinks. "What did your mother want this time?"

"To tell me that Dad's going to be here in two hours. He's been doing business in San Francisco and thought he'd come by and say hello."

"Is this the same dad you and your mother constantly bash?"

"We don't bash him unjustly. I just sympathize with her on the issue of their divorce. Dad's bringing Kathy, by the way."

"His new wife?"

"How many times do I have to tell you? Jessica is his new wife. Kathy is his stepchild."

SIGNS OF DEVOTION

An elderly man is standing at the far end of the pool. He carefully places his towel over a beach chair, his watch on top of the towel, his glasses next to the watch, and his thongs under the chair. Then he makes an imperfect dive into the pool and side-strokes its length. He stands in the water near Della and Frank.

"I heard somewhere that Stephen Sondheim likes to tie people up," Frank says, smiling. "Maybe we could listen to some of his music." If they were getting along, a story like this would cause any tension to melt. Frank would swear on a witness stand that Della has a sense of humor when she wants to.

"What's your source?" Della asks.

The man in the pool appears to be listening. Frank cups his hand over his mouth and whispers something to Della.

"He did not tie you up!" Della says loud enough for the man to hear. "Maybe you wish he would."

Frank rolls his eyes lasciviously.

Della spreads more suntan lotion over her shoulders and onto her thighs.

"You're beautiful when you're angry," Frank says. He reaches to put his hand on her calf.

She slaps it away like she's swatting flies. "Then I must be beautiful all the time since I met you." She closes her eyes. A few minutes later, she says in a different tone of voice, "We should be dressed when they arrive."

"Won't the kid—"

"Kathy is her name."

"Won't Kathy want to swim? When I was a child, that's all I did on vacations. Swim, swim, swim."

Della finishes her glass of mineral water and closes her

DEATH SWAP

eyes. After making herself completely comfortable, she says, "Kathy can swim if she wants. We don't have to all join her. We can sit in chairs like adults and talk to my father. I haven't seen Roland in almost a year."

"What shall we talk about?"

Della doesn't answer. She's decided to take a nap. "Cover your legs if you're going to sleep. They're red as lobsters already."

"Okay, Mom," Frank says, jumping into the pool and swimming twelve laps without stopping.

"I have nothing to wear," Della says, pouting into the mirror.

Frank has put on a long white T-shirt and new jeans with the creases still in them. He's tied back his long hair in a ponytail.

"You look like an ad for the Gap."

"At least I'm ready," Frank says. "He'll be here in twenty minutes."

"How about this?" Della asks and holds up a flowered jersey dress.

"It would show off your tan."

Frank has walked over to where Della's standing. He sits in front of her on the bed wincing up at her face because his legs are so burned.

"I'm not trying to display my tan. I merely want to look presentable." She's put on the flowered dress and is hooking a necklace made of small irregular turquoise and coral beads and tiny bells. It makes a slight tinkling sound as she brushes her hair, applies lipstick and mascara.

"I read there's a new mascara for men that defines your eyelashes without adding color."

"First you want to be tied up and now you covet my make-up. Try to hide your perversity in front of my dad, please."

They're sitting in the nearly empty dining room. It's three o'clock, an off-hour at the lodge, and though they serve "High Tea" from three to five, no one's very interested with the temperature over one hundred degrees.

Her father's dressed in a beige poplin suit. He's wearing a light-blue shirt and a pink-, yellow-, and cream-striped tie. He has Della's thick eyebrows, but his hair is much curlier and mixed with gray. He appears to be amused in advance of anything being said. Della imagines a stranger would call his face sympathetic. Kathy looks like she was manufactured in a different country from her stepfather. Her eyes are light blue and her complexion is pale. Her hair is blond and thin, worn in a blunt cut that ends abruptly at her chin. She's eleven. Kathy's angularity clashes with the table they've chosen. She tries sitting with her elbows on the table. Then she crosses her legs and folds her arms over them on her lap. Then she adjusts her tank top, fiddles with the drawstring of her shorts, cups her chin in one hand and tells the waitress she'll just have Seven-Up. The rest of them have ordered "High Tea." The waitress has brought over a silver-and-glass pastry tray. Roland makes up a small plate for Kathy and suggests she'll want it later. Della watches her father.

"Dad," Kathy says in an exasperated tone familiar to Della. It strikes Della as odd that Kathy also calls this man Dad.

DEATH SWAP

"Your mom tells me you're up here for a week," Roland says. "Any special reason, or just a little break?"

"We thought we'd get away before I start graduate school and Della begins her job," Frank offers.

"You'll be working in the art department?"

"Right, I'll be answering arty phone calls and Xeroxing arty supply orders."

"You never know how you can make use of diverse training later in life. Jessica has a degree in classics, but she's in lobbying now. She writes speeches for environmental lobbies and goes up to Sacramento all the time."

There is a long pause. Della doesn't think that she wants to hear more about Kathy's mom. "What is it you do?" she asks Kathy.

"Not much."

"Kathy's going into sixth grade. She's very good in science and plays the cornet."

"I'm not sure I know what a cornet is," Della says.

"It's a small trumpet," Kathy explains. She holds her fingers in the air and pretends to be playing.

"Frank's in a band," Della offers.

"I play the saxophone." Frank holds an imaginary sax in the air and strains to reach a note. "I started in the Santa Rosa marching band in high school."

"What color was your uniform?" Kathy asks.

"Yeah, what color was it?" says Della.

"Pink with green stripes."

Kathy laughs.

"Really, it was fire-engine red. When I was in the band, I used to pretend that I was playing solos like Sonny Rollins. Probably that's why I wasn't in the band for very long."

SIGNS OF DEVOTION

"I want to be in a marching band someday."

"A noble ambition," Frank smiles.

"I also like games," says Kathy.

"What kind of games?" Della asks.

"Games my dad and I make up."

"Like what?" Della asks.

"There's one we play called Death Swap."

"Sounds spooky," Frank says.

"How does it go?" Della asks. She thinks she's not feeling very well. The light from the windows near the pool looks too bright. The dish of pastries in front of her appears to be swimming in a cloud. Maybe she has to throw up.

"You think of who's dead and who you want back. Like John Lennon."

"Have you read the latest about John Lennon?" Frank asks anyone who's listening. "Seems he liked to pee in people's—"

Della gives Frank a smiting look.

"So who would you take?" Kathy asks Della.

"I don't understand," Della says.

"I offer you someone in exchange for John Lennon. If you accept him, I can have John Lennon."

"How can I give you John Lennon?"

"This is just a game, Della," her father explains. "Kathy doesn't expect you to give her John Lennon."

"So I tell you who'd I'd accept in exchange for John Lennon."

"Right. Like maybe a movie star, or it could be a politician or a sports figure. He has to be just as valuable as John Lennon, though."

"How about Michael Jackson?" Frank says.

"You're not playing. I am," Della says. There is a funny light coming off the silverware. She closes her eyes and blinks twice quickly. She sees that everyone is waiting for her to answer. "My mind is blank," she says. "Besides, how do you make points?"

"You don't. Isn't having John Lennon or John F. Kennedy or Marilyn Monroe back enough?"

"Okay, you give me Dad for John Lennon," Della says.

"You can't use people you know. It gets too personal then."

Della is watching her father's face. A smile is covering it like asphalt.

"That's my final offer, Kathy."

"Della's a real card," Frank is saying. "Why don't we try it again? Let's you and me play, Kathy. I know how to negotiate."

"Okay, who would you give me for the Big Bopper?" Kathy asks.

"How about Dolly Parton?" Frank replies.

"Excuse me," Della says. She thinks she'll go stand by the pool and get some fresh air. The carpeting is swirling at her feet. Her lips are dry and her throat feels closed, as if it'll never swallow again.

The next thing she knows, everyone's standing around her. Frank is putting a cool towel on her forehead. Her father's in a squat, holding her wrist in his hand. Kathy looks like she's trying to hold back tears. "Will she be okay?" Kathy's asking.

"I think she's okay already," Frank explains. "Too much sun can do this to someone."

Della says she'll get up. She staggers over to the nearest table and holds her head in her hands.

"I feel terrible about this," Roland is saying. "I wish I could stay and make it up to you at dinner. I would have liked this visit to have left us all with a better feeling."

Della waves off the comment with her hand. Then her face clears of its misery. "Why don't Frank and I ride back with you?" Della asks. "This vacation isn't working out anyway."

"I don't think that's a good idea, Della. They have a plane to catch in San Francisco."

"Having us in the car won't make them drive any slower, Frank. Besides, I don't feel well. I think it would be better to be in the city if I'm possibly sick."

"Della, it was just the sun. We overdid it outside."

"I'll be happy to drive you back," Roland offers.

Since it's Sunday night, they're caught in an endless line of traffic returning from Wine Country. Kathy and Roland sit in the front seat of the rented Taurus. Frank and Della share the back seat. Della is closing her eyes and leaning her head on Frank's shoulder. Her father is talking to Frank.

"There's lots of room in arts management. You might consider getting a law degree too. Lots of legalese in every field today. Think of how baseball has changed. Someone couldn't have an agent who isn't a lawyer anymore." He waits for Frank's reply.

"He's asleep," Della explains. "Whenever people talk to him about his career, he always falls asleep. He's going to grad school, but he hopes his band will still make it big."

DEATH SWAP

"What do you think was wrong with you, Della? I never saw anyone faint before," Kathy says.

"Probably just the sun, or too much excitement."

"Playing Death Swap isn't that exciting," Roland laughs.

"What's Frank's band's name?" Kathy asks. She unbuckles her seat belt and sits on her knees with her chin perching on top of the headrest so she can see Della better.

"Pardon me, Kathy, but they're called Cock."

Kathy turns around and fastens her seat belt again.

Roland smiles apologetically at Kathy, who has taken a Mad Libs game out of her duffel bag.

"Give me an adjective."

"Straining," Della says.

"This traffic is endless." Roland hums quietly for a minute in the same way Della does when she's nervous. "We should have been back by now. I didn't think it possible that we'd be cutting it close."

"You can drop us anywhere, Dad, as soon as you're back in the city."

At nine-thirty they pull up in front of Frank and Della's apartment, the second floor of a Victorian near Golden Gate Park.

"I wish you could come up," Della tells her dad.

"My next trip," Roland assures. He's unloaded their luggage onto the sidewalk. Standing at the curb, he gives Della a light hug. "Watch that sunburn," he advises.

Della peers into the back window of the car. "I'll wake up Sleeping Beauty."

Kathy smiles broadly.

"Frank!" She opens the door and shakes his arm.

SIGNS OF DEVOTION

Startled awake, Frank sits up and stretches, pulls at his ponytail, realizes they're home and bolts out of the car. He stands on the sidewalk rubbing his eyes with the stupefied look of a child.

Frank and Roland shake hands. Roland embraces Della again and tells her to take it easy for a few days.

"Why did you call your band that gross name?" Kathy asks out of her window before they pull away.

"His last girlfriend suggested it," Della explains, waving good-bye. She watches her dad roll up the car's automatic windows and speed away down the long, sloping street.

"A memorable day," Frank says as he takes a suitcase in either arm up the stairs.

"Who would you give me for Lou Reed?" Della asks when they've reached their landing.

"Lou Reed's not dead yet," Frank says.

"It's good to plan for the future," Della says, hesitating at their door.

HEATHCLIFF

■ ■ ■ ■ ■ ■ ■ ■ ■ Amy is crying for the third time this afternoon. She's sitting on the bay-shaped window seat and looking out at her yard, where Vincent is raking leaves into neat circular piles. Because they've been fighting on and off all day, he's ignoring her. She watches his back, his buttocks, the crease up the back of his pant legs as he leans over to stuff the damp leaves into bags. She glances away when he turns toward the window to look at her. Letting her tears perch on the rims of her eyes before blinking them away, she watches them land on her belly. She calls it a belly now, which is exactly what it is, something convex, something swollen. It's a luxury to cry so much. Talking to the baby inside her, she says, *Daddy is raking leaves.* She has made a promise not to say anything mean about Vincent to the baby.

Vincent's hands smell like soap. He holds her chin in his palms and rubs it like one might polish an apple. "Perk up," he says.

"How can I feel cheery when you said what you did?"

"It was supposed to be a joke." Vincent picks up a tiny clod of dirt that has fallen off his loafers onto the hall runner, and kneads it between his fingers as he sits beside her on the window bench.

She narrows her eyes and asks, "What kind of husband

says, 'I feel as much sympathy for you as I do for any pregnant mammal'?"

"Bambi's mother's husband?" Vincent begins to laugh, a flat, crackly laugh, but when he sees that she hasn't appreciated it, he looks out at the yard and is silent.

The locust tree shakes off a few more miniature leaves. Amy can see that Vincent feels annoyed at the tree. It's making more work for him. He looks like Gregory Peck when he thinks, but she won't tell him that now. She won't please him.

"I'm just saying that we don't have to get sentimental every hour because we're going to be parents. I wouldn't even sit with my parents at the movies. For about fifteen years I would have chosen anyone on earth but them." Vincent tries to take her hand, but Amy withdraws it quickly.

She stares at his familiar knuckles. "That's very sad," she says, shaking her head slowly from side to side and patting her belly. *Isn't that sad?* she asks the baby inside her.

"Or imagine sitting at the park when a smarter, cuter, better-behaved and generally more likable child than your own climbs up the slide. Don't you think that kids can be as disappointing as parents? Let's drop it though, Amy. I have to go out before the stores close."

"Doing some shopping before your eugenics meeting? Tell them we want our *Übermensch* to sleep nights from the start."

"I just need a haircut. I've been waiting all week."

"Can't I go along?"

"Amy," Vincent moans, "it's a haircut."

"Okay. Can you just drop me off on the way?"

"Any old place or a particular destination?"

"I'll go to a movie."

"What movie?"

"Who cares? I want to get out of the house."

Amy blows her nose hard. Vincent takes the Kleenex box from her lap, and before placing it on the counter, hugs her in the exchange.

She goes to the hall closet and, parting ski parkas and folded beach chairs, finds her metallic silver rain slicker, which won't close anymore. Amy lets Vincent pat her belly, then follows him out the door watching his neck, how the childishly fine hair curls up as it grows over his collar. She doesn't understand why they're not angry at each other anymore.

"I think it's depressing to have a baby in December," she says. "Everything will be dead outside." She looks at the geraniums and marigolds trimming her walk. She wonders why the most resilient flowers are so mundane. "Bambi was born in the spring," she continues, but Vincent is already at the car, whisking leaves off the hood, too distant to hear her conciliatory joke.

Whatever movie is playing, she'll see it. She'll buy a large Coke without ice and sit so close that the screen will look as big as an ocean. She'll cry her stupid eyes out again. A few weeks ago when they saw *Passage to India*, the baby's movements accelerated to the martial music. Amy had taken Vincent's hand and had him feel the baby's strident kicks and lunges. She knows that babies belong to you before they are born. She talks to hers in a soft adult voice.

• • •

HEATHCLIFF

"You're in luck. It's a three-hankie special," Vincent says. The marquee reads *Wuthering Heights*. "Call me when it's over and I'll pick you up."

Vincent waves good-bye. He wants a good haircut, close to his ears but long enough in front so that the thinning won't show. Most important, he wants an understanding attitude on part of the barber. Ten weeks ago when his fellowship started, Amy sent him to her hair designer, Dawn, who didn't understand the concept at all.

"You mean you're not working," she said. "I bet Amy's worried, with the baby coming and all."

"They want me to sit home and be creative," he was about to say when the blow-drier started, and Dawn's thin sharp face showed no sign of interest in his intellectual growth.

Now he wants to find a barber who'll appreciate his efforts. Not that he needs the approval of strangers, but he likes people cutting his hair to show a little respect.

"I don't know why you go to Dawn," he'd told Amy later.

His vehemence made her lip curl up in amusement. "Because Dawn can cut my hair in ten minutes. Because she's not interested in Bedouin eating habits."

"Non sequitur."

"Don't you remember that typewriter repairman who wouldn't leave me alone once he discovered that I'd lived in Africa?"

"No," he had said just to be peevish. Amy had been in the Peace Corps right after college. She'd introduced soybeans to an area of the Sudan where they were unsuited to grow. Whenever Vincent wants to feel tender about Amy, he thinks of the shriveling vines she lovingly tended for a year.

SIGNS OF DEVOTION

Now he is in front of a regulation-looking barbershop. An elderly man is sleeping in a marbled red barber's chair. He wears the high-collared medicinal-blue shirt of a dentist or a pharmacist. The sign outside says "Lucky's."

When Vincent opens the door, an old-fashioned bell rings. Vincent remembers that same ringing from his childhood. He connects it with the acrid smell of a dry cleaner's store that also sold candy, kite string, and eyeglass chains.

Lucky slouches to his feet. He appears to be surprised at the heaviness of his own body. "Hi," he says.

Vincent feels relieved that this is going to be easy. "I need a haircut." He smiles the gratuitous smile of a potential victim.

"Sit down." Lucky fixes a rough terry towel around Vincent's neck with a barber clip. Vincent wonders how a one-man barbershop can keep Lucky in clean towels.

"Busy today?"

"Oh, sure."

He's no talker. Vincent can see himself looking straight ahead in the curved mirror. Behind him are three empty red armchairs, where customers can wait.

"I get the regulars," Lucky adds.

"Steady customers."

"Right. A man down the street comes in. He's nearly blind, but once a week I trim his hair and do a lot for his ears. Lots of hair in them. He wants to be sure *they're* working. He's in on Tuesdays."

Vincent wonders if that's Lucky's only regular customer. "Well, I'm in the neighborhood, but I usually get my hair cut at the university." He tries not to look at himself as he lies. When Lucky doesn't respond, Vincent continues, "I'm

■ 51

off this semester researching a book on economics. My wife is off too because she'll be having a baby soon."

"I don't cut children's hair. They won't sit still, not for a minute. I tell their mothers or fathers, 'These are dangerous tools I use.'" He snips the air for emphasis. "But they don't care."

"Been in business long?"

"Thirty-seven years. Right out of the army I started working for Lucky. His heart got bad, so he moved to New Mexico about six years ago. I still think he'd have done better in Florida. He's died since. You know how it is."

"So your name's not Lucky?"

"I'm Dennis."

"Why not call it Dennis's?"

"Why change now?"

In the long silence that follows, Dennis finishes the haircut, shaves Vincent's neck, dusts his collar line from an ancient yellowed container of talc, and holds a head-shaped mirror up to his head.

"Looks fine."

At six he picks Amy up at the movie. She is waiting outside studying the marquee when he pulls up. Her rain slicker looks like a child's. Her profile is more poignant than he wants to acknowledge. "Hey, pregnant lady, want a ride?"

She climbs in slowly and crosses her legs. Her arms encircle her belly. "Who cut your hair?"

"Not Lucky."

"If not Lucky, then who?"

"Dennis, but he won't cut children's hair, so don't ask."

"All right."

"How was the movie?"

"We liked it," Amy says. Laurence Olivier was a beautiful man." She's quiet for a minute. "How about naming the baby Heathcliff?"

"Wasn't Heathcliff an orphan?"

"That's my point," Amy says. "You don't want to have a child, do you?"

Vincent feels overcome by sadness. He remembers a summer in Greece when he and his parents had three hours on Mykonos before their tour boat was going to leave. Walking in the late-afternoon heat down a typical lane with its white houses and blue-washed doorways, they saw a parlor in which an elderly mother, father, and a son about Vincent's age were watching TV. A calico cat was perched on the set, on which Cuba was playing the United States in Olympic basketball. Sometimes its tail swished over the screen, and their view was obscured. Vincent saw that his father looked moved, and asked him if something was wrong. His father had said, "Look at how small the world's become, son." Vincent knew he'd meant more: that they could have been this family, discovered by chance in the middle of an ocean; that soon, since Vincent was graduating college, he would never live with his parents again.

Vincent pulls over two blocks before their house and turns off the car engine.

"What are you doing?" Amy asks.

"I'm too sad to drive," he says, pressing his body toward Amy and nuzzling her neck.

HEATHCLIFF

"What are you sad about?"

"Families."

"I know," Amy says. "But our family will be different. No one will ever get old. Our children will always love us. We'll send those silly letters at Christmas that report on Jimmy's art project and Nora's braces."

They both laugh uneasily.

Amy looks into the picture window of the red Georgian across the lawn. The front room is lit by the blue iridescence of a television screen. Amy can see an older woman standing in front of the window facing several others seated on a couch. The woman is waving her hands up and down, her fingers moving in graceful sweeps in and out of the light.

"Look!" she whispers to Vincent. "She's leading them all in a song."

"That's what I mean," Vincent says. "Look at that old woman. She thinks that what she's doing is private, but we're watching her, Amy, and the people she's commanding to do this or that are watching her too. People will watch us be parents, and they'll judge. And how will we know if we're right or they're right?"

"Why are you assuming we'll be at odds?"

"Because no one ever understands, Amy. You don't have to lock your children up or abuse them. You just have to be their parents to do something wrong. You're bound to slip up. My parents were kind, but they slipped up constantly in so many ways. It can't be helped."

"Listen," Amy says, putting Vincent's hands on her heaving belly. "The baby is talking to you. What is he saying?"

"I don't know, Amy. Is this a séance?"

"He's saying that he understands. That he forgives you already. He's saying he's glad to know you."

Vincent starts the car. He opens his mouth but doesn't say anything.

Amy wonders whether he has accepted her benediction. Later, when she bathes in the lion's-claw tub that she's grown nearly too large to fit, she'll apologize to the baby for telling this necessary lie.

THE STOCKHOLM SYNDROME

■ ■ ■ ■ ■ ■ ■ ■ ■ It isn't right for a woman with one breast, a woman anyone would call matronly, to go on vacation, meet a man, and never come home. That's what Clarice did last summer, and all I have is a postcard to hint at a reason. I blame Buddy, who made her life difficult at home. She once told us why the book club could never meet at her house. "Buddy doesn't want his privacy invaded," she apologized, jokingly. Maybe he would have to throw on a clean shirt for us or help Clarice serve the refreshments. Maybe he would have to say more than hello. Not that he was a bad kid, but he was a kid for too long.

Clarice would come to our book club meetings prepared, ready as anyone to discuss whatever it was we were reading. One week, long before it became a movie with that sad sack William Hurt, it was *The Accidental Tourist.* Clarice was the presenter, which is how we work it. We take turns. One month Shirley does it, one month Irene, one month it's me, and then Clarice. It's no little thing to be a presenter. Irene, for one, gets a new dress when it's her turn. I remember one Tuesday last March when she looked radiant. It was her turn to lead us in *The Life of Patty Hearst.* I for one wouldn't trade Patty Hearst's millions for her rotten life. But that's another story. Irene was wearing a black rayon suit with little white dots by Nina Piccalino. But what I remember most is how passionate Clarice got defending the

THE STOCKHOLM SYNDROME

girl. She said she might do anything for a lover, like Patty Hearst did. We asked if he'd have to lock her in a closet, and she said no. There's just a time in your life when things are right to do, and I guess when Clarice went to California was one of them.

She was sixty-seven, which means that Buddy's thirty-seven. Now I believe in strong family ties, but Buddy's not a regular kid. He's been known to take advantage. I've known Clarice so long that I remember Buddy as a child. Kids can get clingy when a father dies, but even before Abe passed, it was Buddy needs this and Buddy needs that and Buddy can't do this or that for himself. That's why that particular book-club meeting on *The Accidental Tourist* is so memorable. Clarice is in the middle of making an important point about one of Macon's brothers. Shirley's in the middle of disagreeing, and the phone rings. It's Buddy. He's locked himself out of the house, and Clarice is supposed to leave the book club to let him in. We can tell she's embarrassed. The discussion isn't half over, and she has to excuse herself because a grown man can't hold on to his keys or hang out in a bar until she's expected home. She says it won't take more than twenty minutes and she's right. At two-twenty she's back, and I really must commend the way she picked up the discussion right where she left off. The sad part was that we were about four chapters ahead, but nobody had the heart to tell her.

One of Clarice's arms is always swollen from the operation she had some years ago. She's a thin woman with a pretty face and clear blue eyes. We call her Einstein, not because she's a genius but because of her hair. I bet when she was little, someone was always telling her to fix her crazy

SIGNS OF DEVOTION

hair. It's the kind of short hair that looks long and wild. She has a nice figure and dresses well. You can't tell except for her arm that she's had the breast removed. I can see how a man would be interested in her face. She'd usually wear full sleeves, but sometimes she'd see a nice suit or dress and just buy it. If she can live with her arm, anyone should be able to. I wonder if the man she met noticed the arm or not. I think about it because Clarice is shy, and I worry about their first time in bed if he didn't know.

She sent me a postcard of Chinatown after she decided to stay in San Francisco. Now years ago, I was in that same Chinatown with my family. We were in a restaurant that serves dim sum, those little dumplings with different fillings, and damned if a little Chinese girl doesn't pass us with a cartful of cooked duck's feet. They are as yellow as the sun, and one of my little ones, Andrea, screams. She was a real sensitive kid. If she saw a bug smashed on a windshield, she'd cry. Having three brothers didn't make it any easier for her. One of them was always hurting something by accident, of course. If there was a cat around, its tail might get slammed in a door, or if there were goldfish, maybe one of the boys would leave the bowl in the sun on an early September afternoon. Their water would get so hot they'd be cooked by the end of school, and poor little Andrea would come in and discover them. So it was really too bad that even on our vacation she couldn't get away from it all. Clarice never sent photos of duck's feet. She sent a bright-red pagoda, and the message was short: "I'm so happy with Keith that I've decided to stay." Well, if she's happy, I'm happy too, but getting that message made me wonder. You'd think she might have called, but sweethearts like their privacy.

THE STOCKHOLM SYNDROME

When the postcard came, I phoned Irene. I wondered if we should visit Buddy and inquire after his health. Here's a boy, a grown man, really, but every creature comfort has always been given him. He gets three square meals a day and a warm place to sleep. Putting it that way makes it sound like he's living in a kennel, but you know what I mean. He doesn't have to struggle like the rest of us. Clarice has some money, Buddy has a good man managing his dad's old business, and things are fine. Maybe he meets a girl now and then, but it's never serious enough to replace Clarice.

First Irene says we shouldn't meddle. If Buddy's unhappy, Clarice is sure to know. But I say it's the kind thing to do. Suppose Clarice died. Wouldn't we look after Buddy for her? From Buddy's point of view, Clarice's moving away might not be much different from her dying. So Irene agrees. If I call Buddy and he wants to see us, she'll come along.

I try reaching Buddy for about four nights without much luck. It's a Friday night when I finally get him on the line.

"Buddy," I say. "It's Mrs. Riess." Not that I'd mind him calling me Margaret, but he's always called me Mrs. Riess.

I hear him turning down the television in the background and saying hello at the same time. He doesn't sound all that glad to hear from me.

"Irene and I were hoping you're fine. We wanted to say hello." He doesn't say a word, so I'm going on like this. I even tell him the story about the duck's feet before he says much of anything.

He asks me how my kids are. I give him the summary, though I spare some details about Andrea's divorce. That's a topic I try to avoid. It's better for my health. I ask him if he needs anything, and he says he would like to talk to us, meaning me and Irene, and says why not come by tomorrow about four.

When I tell Irene that he wants to see us, I'm surprised at how she reacts. She has no curiosity or confidence, I'm not sure which. She says in her twitchy little voice that Saturday's really a bad day for her, and she already has plans, and about a hundred other things that don't make sense. She uses up every alibi she's ever contrived for this one meeting with a boy of no consequence. I tell her I'll go alone, and she says she promised to go and will try to live up to it.

I've known Irene forever. Even when we were kids, things used to intimidate her. There was a teacher who was crazy. You could have had Miss Nichols certified. It terrified her to be touched. She'd shout things at children like, "Look what you've done! You've made a run in my stockings!" when someone stepped on her toe. We'd intentionally jostle her just to see her face turn red and her eyes get small with anger. But not Irene. Irene spent fifth grade watching extra-carefully where she stepped. Once, as a prank, Bobby Roeder pushed Irene into Mrs. Nichols. "We should watch where we land!" Miss Nichols screeched, knowing full well as a teacher that objects crashing through space don't have a will of their own.

Irene honks for me at three forty-five. I'm already out on the porch waiting. I've bought some bakery cookies to take Buddy, and Irene, the one who doesn't want to go, has baked a marble pound cake. It's sitting between us on the front seat of her Ford. Irene's a slow driver, so we arrive about twenty minutes later, when it should take ten.

We wait a long time at the door before Buddy answers. I expect to find a mess in the house, but the front room's immaculate, and Buddy has laid out some fancy pastries and nice mugs for coffee. He's ground the coffee in a special machine, and it smells much better than the instant I've come to use. Buddy seems to have a house guest too, a nice younger man named Dave. Dave is in the kitchen when we come in, and his sleeves are pulled up to his elbows, and his hands are in the sink. He's washing dishes. It's not remarkable because men are different these days. They take care of things if they have to.

We sit in the front room. Buddy and I are on the couch. Irene's in a light-blue easy chair, and when Dave finishes in the kitchen and we're still making small talk, he joins us too.

"Nice of you to come," Dave says, like we're here to see him, and I begin to wonder if Dave is more than a friend.

"Do you hear from your mom?" I ask Buddy.

"They talk all the time," Dave says. "You should see our phone bill."

The way he says "our phone bill" clears a few things up for me. "I bet you're glad to have Dave around now that your mom's away," I tell Buddy.

I look at Irene, and she's digging a hole in her coffee cup with her spoon. She won't look at me no matter what I do.

"Dave lived here before Mom left," Buddy tells me. "She's happy out there, and I'm happy here."

"So everybody's happy," I add. I look around the walls of the room. There's a lot of Indian art and some is frankly erotic. I wonder if Dave's an anthropologist. "So what do you do for a living?" I ask him.

"I'm a dog groomer," he says. "We met when Buddy still

had Bridget. Bridget, their poodle, has been dead for almost a decade. I know that because Bridget died before Rudy, my little collie.

"And you've lived here all these years?" I ask.

"Only a few months," Dave explains. And he shoots this little smile that's only meant for Buddy through the room.

"Have you met Keith?" I ask Buddy.

"The mysterious Keith? No, but he sounds very nice on the phone. He's a retired math teacher. Do you know how they met? Mom went to a Scrabble club, and they played each other in a semi-final round."

"Who won?" I ask, and Buddy says he doesn't know. I think it's strange that he doesn't know the outcome of a story he must tell again and again, but some people are just naturally curious and some are not.

Now Irene, who's been as quiet as can be, pipes up. She doesn't say she likes their furniture or anything normal. "I think it's the Stockholm Syndrome," Irene says.

Plunk, the words just lie there. She's back to stirring her coffee and choosing another pastry. I know what she's talking about, but does she expect me to do all the explaining?

Finally Dave says politely, "Excuse me, but what's that?" It figures he doesn't know about the Stockholm Syndrome, being a dog groomer. It's not like a dog groomer can't listen to the news, but he probably doesn't go in for the big issues like me and Irene and the rest of us in the club.

Of course Irene doesn't answer. There's a moment of silence that makes everyone flinch, and then I say, "It's when captives fall in love with their captors. Like Patty Hearst having a love affair with that man who raped her."

THE STOCKHOLM SYNDROME

The men exchange glances. I bet they don't expect old women, friends of Buddy's mother, to talk that way. I wasn't trying to be shocking. I was just trying to explain what they asked.

"So you think my mother's being held against her will?"

"Pardon me," I say, "but I was just elaborating for Irene."

That puts Irene on the spot, so she pipes up for once. "This man beats your mother, a very good Scrabble player, and then they fall in love. It doesn't have to be physical, how people overpower you. Keith subdued your mother, and now she thinks she loves him." Her mouth snaps shut like an electronic door.

Two things come to my mind. Dave and Buddy haven't asked why it's named after Stockholm. If either of them were really thinking, he'd have asked. And why is it that Irene thinks Clarice lost at Scrabble? No one said a thing about her losing. "Buddy, did Clarice lose?" I ask.

"She didn't say." Then he's quiet for a second. "But if she didn't say, I'd guess she did lose." Buddy and Dave share a big laugh because they've thought of the same thing at the same time. I remember laughing like that with Norman before the kids were born. I try to smile at Irene about Buddy's conclusion, but it's not the same.

I see that it's getting late outside and these two men are probably busy, so I tell Irene we'd better go.

"Why do they call it the Stockholm Syndrome?" Dave asks before we're out the door. Hoping Irene will do some of the work, I'm quiet. We stand there still as statues until I say that Stockholm's the place that hostages go to get deprogrammed. Buddy makes some joke about a clinic that breaks hearts, and we all laugh at that. I don't know if

Stockholm's a romantic place, I'm thinking, but there are all kinds of love, that's for sure.

Dave shakes my hand and then takes Irene's hand in his to say good-bye. Watching Irene's tentative smile, I think of crazy old Miss Nichols.

As soon as we're in the car, Irene sighs. I'm used to her making that same sigh after sixty years, but it says so little that I'm wondering why she's satisfied with it anymore.

SAVING THE AUSTRALIAN ELEPHANT

Barry and Joan made a perfect olfactory pair. He smelled nothing, she everything. She told him how the logs smelled on the fire. On the morning that he decided to leave, she didn't tell him that their dinner of mussels the night before had left an unpleasant odor in the kitchen. I have this information on the testimony of Joan. Few times are we privy to turning points in people's lives. Mostly we hear about them later and sometimes unintentionally.

Although I hardly knew Joan, her story has become the unifying theme of my week in Australia. If someone other than my boss asks me what I accomplished there, I'll say, "I learned about Joan."

Let's start at the beginning, though. I heard many conversations during my week in Sydney. I'd get on the bus, pay my fare, gauged by the distance I was to travel, and knowing no one and having little to do, listen to people around me.

One morning an elderly couple said this:

He: Frank's a good man.

She: So is she.

He: They have one child?

She: They have five!

I decided that many couples, me and my ex-wife included, were like the bus passengers, unable to agree on the simplest details of living.

SAVING THE AUSTRALIAN ELEPHANT

Another thing the elderly couple said was that the African elephant was in danger. The husband wondered whether that was the elephant with the larger or smaller ears. The wife said she didn't know. Moreover, she added, as long as the elephants in Australia were fine, she didn't much care what happened to them in Africa.

I had recently visited the Taronga Zoo, where, along with German honeymooners, I'd taken a monorail to the top of the path leading down to the giant-panda exhibit from China. From what I know of German, it seems the couple were having a spirited argument about structuralism. As the husband tried to direct her attention to the lush pathways below, where ibises strolled like Sunday tourists, the woman made her final point. "Barthes," she said, kohl-lined eyes squinting in fervor, "ist sehr alt." The husband laughed and mussed her hair in affection, but I detected the tension. In any case, their knees seemed to point aggressively at me, and I was glad when our ride ended.

The pandas were sleeping when my turn came to view them. Maybe if I could have stayed longer, one would have lumbered to its feet and at least munched perfunctorily on some bamboo. Because the animals were so inactive, I spent most of my time observing the working-class Australian couple who'd taken their children, all wearing ornate cowboy boots, to see the exhibit. They were in an ill humor and frequently slapped their youngest son for disobeying, which included bumping into me. I didn't mind that the little boy was unaware of where his family ended and I began. I thought of telling the parents so, but I'm careful not to interfere in the order of things when I travel. This is a conscious decision based on the time when I removed a sleeping tortoise from a median strip in West Virginia and set it safely in the grass by the roadside. After I'd driven away, I was haunted by misgivings. Had I placed him on the wrong side of the road, ruining his life forever?

I had noticed that the elephants in the Taronga Zoo looked very healthy. The trainer put them through their paces, and the female elephant, who was especially obliging, stood on a barrel and balanced on one foot. She was very calm about it. From what I could gather, the woman on the bus was right in assuming that her own elephants were content. They had nothing to fear from society encroaching or poachers killing off the large males to obtain their tusks.

At day's end, I'd take the long bus ride to Stanmore and recount my adventures to Joan. When I told her what I had heard on the bus and in the monorail, she chose not to reply. Later that night, when I was sitting at her kitchen table planning my next day's activities, she told me what she really thought about zoos. She herself wouldn't visit one, considering how the animals were imprisoned and exploited. She wondered if zoos weren't built so that Americans, the spoiled children of the globe, could feel at home wherever they traveled.

I told her I hadn't had a particularly good time at the zoo myself, what with the sleeping pandas and cruel parents, but that my own experience couldn't serve as proof of a definitive attitude on the part of all Americans. She went on to recount what an American family viewing koala bears had once said: "Look at how tame they are. They look stuffed." What they had said was ordinary enough. It was the manner in which she imitated them that was remarkable. Joan prided herself on reproducing American accents.

SAVING THE AUSTRALIAN ELEPHANT

The previous night I had stayed with her, she'd done an impression of Edward Kennedy talking to Jimmy Stewart, but her Boston dialect left much to be desired. I watched as it pulled her face askew and left her quite exhausted.

I finally began wondering what the real story was behind Barry's leaving Joan, not that I knew Barry or even took much interest in Joan. Just for the sake of truth, I began questioning if what drove them apart had anything to do with her false estimation of her abilities. Maybe she as well as Barry had a poor sense of smell, and several times a day people had to tell them embarrassing facts about themselves. Maybe they sat side by side on a bus discussing magnolias or marinara sauce, and a tourist such as I found himself interrupting their conversation to tell them that the calamari they were carrying home for dinner was causing more than a little unpleasantness for the other passengers. If this had happened too often, I'd imagine it could have placed quite a strain on even the best relationship.

The next morning, before I began the negotiations for which my firm had sent me to Sydney, I told Joan I wanted to take a walk in the Royal Botanical Gardens. My guidebook said they crest several hills facing the harbor.

"I'll draw you a map," Joan offered. "The gardens are quite large." She sat down at her desk and quickly produced a detailed document. She used a calligraphic pen. The arrow she drew to indicate north seemed capable of flight.

From the map Joan had drawn me, I should have been able to see the art museum after approximately ten minutes of brisk walking from where the cab left me. After nearly half an hour of roaming through large uncultivated tracts and wondering whether I was even in the gardens proper anymore, I crossed paths with a tall middle-aged man and his three sons. All I wanted was to be directed toward the main gate, where I'd get a cab to go to my noon meeting. The man was wearing shorts, a good indication of his Australian origins. He was down from Brisbane for the day, and confessed that he, too, was lost. We marched on like a flock of geese, he leading, until we found a young bearded gardener who showed us on Joan's map where the main gates were.

"And the art museum?" I asked out of curiosity.

He pointed to a place off the map near my elbow.

"So my map is inaccurate?" I added, feeling as if I were already involved in the negotiating process.

"It's a travesty," the gardener said and laughed robustly, displaying handsome teeth.

As I'd expected, the contract was easy to negotiate. Both parties had lots of money to make from the deal, so I was less a lawyer than a courier of goodwill. The firm always anticipated problems that never arose, so I had two more days to spend in Sydney.

That night I greeted Joan and said nothing about my troubles in the garden. I was grateful for my free lodgings with this woman, who was a college friend of my ex-wife's new husband. When Joan asked me how I had liked the aboriginal exhibit, I couldn't lie, of course.

"I never got there," I told her, thinking I'd drop it at that.

She exhaled air through her mouth, enough to blow a smoke ring if she had been smoking a cigarette. This was her expression of disgust, meaning I was a damned nuisance for not going to the exhibit after she'd gone to the trouble of drawing the map for me.

SAVING THE AUSTRALIAN ELEPHANT

I suggested that I take her to dinner at that point, hoping the discussion would end. She was rather pretty in a plain sort of way. She looked like a drawing of simple beauty, one that a fourteen year-old-girl might make. There was nothing complicated about her looks, but her imprecision, which might lead ships to icebergs, was unfathomable to me.

She wouldn't let it drop at that. "I don't know why I bother," she said.

"If you mean the map, it was way out of proportion. Not only could I not find the museum, but I couldn't find a damned Australian who lived in Sydney to direct me out of the gardens." I stopped there, short of telling her about the gardener who'd called her map a travesty.

I heard her drawing a bath in the next room. She stayed in there for a long time and came out dripping wet in a blue terry robe and Swedish clogs whose scuffing anticipated her arrival into the room. I could see that she'd been crying.

"I'm sorry," she said.

"No, I owe you an apology."

"I used to get things right all the time before Barry left," she said. "Do you know what I do for a living?"

I knew she was an engineer of some sort, but I didn't want to sound like a wise guy. "No, what?" I asked.

"I design fucking highways," she said, pronouncing it like "eyeways." Then she made some tea. She used milk in hers, so I decided to have mine the same way.

"To highways," I toasted, raising my teacup.

We took the ferry to Mosman Bay and back to the harbor. From the boat you could see the botanical gardens, and beyond that, the museum I hadn't been able to locate.

"Do you still have my instructions?" she asked.

Without thinking, I said yes, and unfolded them from my pocket.

She laughed. It was a preface to anything that might follow. In the waning light of the evening, she studied the sheet with great purpose, eyes squinting. She shook her head in dismay.

"You might just throw it overboard," I said.

"I spoke to Barry today. He says he's interested in trying it again."

"That's wonderful," I said, thinking that my presence in her house had incited her to call and ask him back. Had I caused chasms to fill with regret for lost chances? I pictured the Grand Canyon overflowing with silt as I stood grinning at its rim. To make conversation, I said, "I'm sure Brian will be happy to hear that."

"Who's Brian?" she asked, puzzled.

"My ex-wife's new husband. Your friend from NYU, remember?"

"Brian never met Barry. He won't care in the least." Then she looked up at the sky so different in this hemisphere that I couldn't chart the stars at all. "How could your wife have preferred Brian to you?"

That surprised me enough that I decided to kiss her. When I opened my eyes again, I saw a Greek couple staring at us. I wondered if they knew any English. "Why do you say that about Brian?" I asked.

"He was such a thug in college. He'd batter down everyone's defenses with his smug intelligence, and just when we all wearied of listening, he'd dare to be utterly mundane. I guess that's American, huh?"

"Am I like that?" I asked.

"No, you seem more reticent, almost British. You turn a map upside down and think it leads you nowhere. I find that more British."

She was holding the map now, and before I could grab it from her, she tossed it into the harbor.

"You know what my son used to call our galaxy?" I said. "Australia's in the same galaxy as we are, is it not?"

"What?" she asked, still flushed with the thrill of destroying evidence.

"He used to say we live in the Easy Way. Instead of the Milky Way," I added in case she hadn't understood.

She took my hand and pointed it toward the sky. "That's the Southern Cross," she said, tracing four lights above us. Then she smiled at me. It was crazy, but for a second I thought that she'd done a perfect imitation of my voice.

■ ■ ■ ■ ■ ■ ■ ■ ■ ■ ■ ■ ■ ■ ■ ■ ■ ■

KEYS

■ ■ ■ ■ ■ ■ ■ ■ ■ When Ellen's mother was dying three winters ago, she won the first prize of her life, a stuffed elephant toy, in a holiday-bazaar raffle. When she phoned me to ask if I'd pick up the gift for her, I asked why she hadn't called Ellen.

"Ellen has her own problems," Grace told me. "I hate to hear about them. And I figure that I've known you almost as long as my own daughter." She reminded me of the time she had taken me on the parachute ride, the most terrifying ride at Riverview, three times in the summer of 1960. Ellen, who was afraid of anything but the merry-go-round and a spinning pink teacup ride, had laughed from the sidelines.

I didn't know if Grace knew that Ellen had told me about her illness. If I wasn't supposed to know, why would I be so eager to help? If I was to know, what should I say to the woman when I dropped off the toy? I decided to call Ellen and ask her what her mother knew about my knowing her situation. Ellen's son Adam answered. He'd be an excellent solution to the elephant problem, I thought at the time.

"Adam," I asked. "Did you hear that your grandmother won a toy elephant?"

"So?"

The word stretched out in front of me. It opened caverns of pity I never thought a word capable of holding. "So your grandma is sick and she won an elephant," I told the little brat. "And I assume you don't want the thing because she's asked me instead of your mom to bring it to her. Is this situation familiar to you or not?"

"My mom's not talking to Grandma, at least not really."

"What does 'really' mean?" I asked him. Was he suggesting they talk officially but that a call about a gift would be construed as unofficial?

"Sometimes Mom talks to Grandma's doctor, but she never talks to Grandma. I think it has something to do with Rex."

I still thought of a dog when I heard Rex's name, but instead of a dog I forced myself to picture the stooped paleontologist for whom Ellen had left a perfectly capable husband, now known in conversation as "Adam's father."

"How's Adam's father?" I'd ask Ellen, wanting some news of John.

Misunderstanding my question, Ellen would tell me that he more than willingly paid child support and that he'd never canceled a Sunday visit. It seemed there was no way to access the file labeled "John Cantos," at least not without Ellen's editing it so severely that its contents would be suspect anyway.

"He felt disdain for what he'd made me," was the line I remembered best. I thought of the lesson in perspective from my high school math book. A man in a fedora receded down a seemingly endless railroad track. Though he appeared to be standing in front of me, I knew I'd never shake his hand or arrive close to the point in space where I might touch his imagined lapel.

After speaking to Adam, I realized I was alone with the

prize. I'd deliver the stuffed elephant without further reflection on John, Ellen, Adam, or the nature of memory.

Dinner that night was at Celeste's apartment. I couldn't help conjuring up Babar's wife posed with her back to the audience and dressed as a bride on the last page of my childhood book. This Celeste, however, was a bench-pressing lesbian, our former neighbor, who only invited us over after a lover had jilted her or a job lead had fizzled. Her indifference to cuisine bordered on fanaticism. In fact, we had met when she had knocked on our condo door, asking to borrow salt and a can opener.

"I wanted to cook an Iranian dish, but I couldn't get the kind of yogurt I needed," Celeste said as she placed a tureen of grayish soup in front of us.

I tried not to look at Charles, who takes dining seriously. When the pressure of shared speechlessness pressed too heavily, I finally asked him, "Why do you look so abject?" His response was a kick under the table, which meant that he didn't like dinner, and a question to Celeste about Salman Rushdie and the Ayatollah. I remembered one evening when Charles had sulked over his bouillabaisse, while Ellen and I sucked the meat out of our crab legs. "Let's share," I finally told him to preserve our marriage and our credibility in Ellen's eyes.

"I'm just thinking about sadness," Charles said.

"As a cause or an effect?" Celeste questioned.

When Charles said, "As effect," they both exhaled together. It was a strange moment of misunderstood empathy. While Charles was picturing rack of lamb and new potatoes, I'm sure Celeste was seeing the face of Renata, a book-

KEYS

store manager who'd been her lover until late last Thursday. I felt a strange tingling in my face. The trouble with red hair is how easily you blush. I plunged my spoon into the concoction with new vigor, hoping the moment would pass.

When we had finished the still-frozen cheesecake, Celeste started crying softly. "I look like a bear," she managed.

"What do you mean?" Charles asked.

"Look at me. I'm all muscled and hairy. Weight lifting is supposed to make me sleek."

What could we say? Charles told Celeste that we're all getting older. He forced her to pinch his midriff. "Go ahead," he said, pushing his chest in her direction. "See what I mean?"

I told her not to worry, that potential lovers are everywhere. Furthermore, we all resemble animals.

We turned the rest of the evening into a parlor game involving our animal identities. Gerald Ford, political affiliations aside, was an elephant. Sammy Davis, Jr., was a ferret. We all agreed that Johnny Carson was a definite prairie dog.

Celeste noticed that animal characterization seemed easier with men. I suggested that Meryl Streep resembled a lizard.

"No more than William Buckley," Charles added to be difficult.

The evening finally ended with kisses at the door and promises that we'd send any women resembling baby harp seals Celeste's way.

"Where do you think she got a name like that?" I asked Charles on the way to the car.

SIGNS OF DEVOTION

"That was another problem all evening. The food aside, I couldn't remember her goddamn name."

"Babar's wife."

"Huh?"

"Celeste."

The building where Grace's prize awaited me resembled an asphalt-siding rendition of an Argyle sock. I entered the unmarked door and went to a reception desk, where a woman sat stamping invoices. I wondered if I needed a coupon to redeem Grace's elephant or whether it would be surrendered without complaint.

"I've come to pick up a stuffed elephant that a Mrs. Pankrot won in a raffle."

"Frank, look in the prize box," the clerk said without looking up. Did I need to explain that it wasn't for me? I stood there quite a long time trying to guess exactly where I was. Obviously it was a business, but what kind of business? Did they make stuffed elephants here, or was that ancillary to something more serious, say, the manufacturing of Ditto supplies?

After several minutes a man presented me with a yellowed plastic bag the size of a piece of carry-on luggage. Inside was an unadorned elephant doll. No hat, coat, tie or shoes. No tail that I could see. I wondered if Mrs. Pankrot would notice the missing tail as I tossed the toy into my back seat.

Mrs. Pankrot lived in the third geriatric high-rise on the block. The building was called "The Breakers," as I read on a large billboard when I parked my car. I pictured two tough

KEYS

guys, movers with rolled-up sleeves, ready to help little old women grocery-shop or move their furniture to dust under a difficult corner. I considered leaving the prize with the doorman, but that would have disappointed Grace, who must be lonely for conversation to have called me in the first place.

She had prepared a little snack for us. On a card table in the living room directly in front of the console television was a loaf of banana bread, sugar and cream in matching crystal bowls, and a pot of tea warmed inside a paisley tea cozy. I was to sit on the "good chair," as Grace called the matching card-table chair. She seated herself slowly on the couch that hugged the longest wall in the apartment. Above it was a Winslow Homer painting. Apparently I was to eat alone.

She didn't have much to say to me while I used my fingers to break off pieces of banana bread and sloshed them down with tea. When she talked at all, her comments were on my eating habits. She didn't think it was healthy that I took my tea black. Two lumps was how she always drank hers. She thought that maybe she should have provided butter for the bread, but with what we know about butter, it's like helping a guest kill herself.

I began to feel self-conscious eating alone, but I assumed that her not partaking had something to do with her illness and was hesitant to ask.

After I pushed away from the table, which proved to be the signal she was waiting for, she began. "The year that Ellen left John, she changed her key chain four times. For nine years they are married, and she has the same chain all the time. Then comes year ten and every time I see Ellen, it's something new. First she has one that looks like a fist. Then it's a big ribbon made out of metal. Then she has one that looks like a little shoe. Before then, you always knew it would be a plain silver ring. I know she has to be up to monkey business to change her keys so many times."

She cleared her throat, waiting for me to answer. Putting a pillow behind her neck, she closed her eyes for a moment, scratched her head vigorously and looked at me with disappointment.

"When you're fiddling with keys, you break things. It's that simple."

She opened her arms wide in a satisfied pose and smiled, mostly with her eyes.

"I brought the elephant. It's on the bed with my coat."

"You want it?" she asked.

"Thank you, Grace, but after all, you won it," I said rather tentatively. Was it sadder to picture her keeping the thing, or me driving away with it in my back seat?

"Maybe you know a child," she added.

"How about Adam?" I asked.

She closed her eyes for a long time. It was as if the curtain had come down, ending the first act of an opera. When she opened them again, she had changed subjects.

"Do you and Charles still travel so much?"

"Less now," I told her. "Charles used to have to go to England almost every month. Now we get away maybe twice a year."

"Where did you go recently?" she asked.

"Let's see. We spent two nights in Salt Lake City, but you mean something different, right?"

"Once, when Ellen was just a baby, Jordan and I went to

KEYS

Cape Cod to see the sights. There was a flag or placard at one point, I can't remember which, that said, 'This is the spot in the United States closest to Europe.'"

"Did you get to Europe?" I asked.

"The funny thing was," she continued, "that I didn't even consider that the sign had anything to do with me. I was Ellen's mother. That was a sign about geography." She folded her hands and sighed. "Knowing what I know now, I should have started swimming."

She laughed at her joke for a long time. I sat there wishing that Grace had won a better prize. I thought about what I had in my purse to give her, but nothing came to mind.

"So you must be a busy girl," she said. "I won't keep you much longer." She got up slowly, marched into the bedroom, and came back holding the elephant still wrapped in plastic. She unwrapped it with great energy and sat it next to her on the couch. It was the cheap kind of stuffed animal that would lose an eye in maybe a week.

"Does Ellen know I won a prize?" she asked.

"I called but Adam answered."

She shifted on the pillows and stroked her hair, troubled by the news.

"That boy's like his mother."

"He does favor her," I agreed, knowing she meant something completely different.

"Give it to him when you see him," she said, handing me the toy. "How do you say what it would mean if I kept it? That it would be too ironic?"

"I guess that's the word."

"Funny that there's a word for an old woman who would want to keep an elephant."

ELEMENT 109

■ ■ ■ ■ ■ ■ ■ ■ ■ My good old friend Kenneth just turned forty-one, yet he insists on dating women who are twenty. That means they were born after Sonny and Cher fell from prominence. My brother and I, twelve and ten, respectively, used to dress in Neanderthal fur vests and join forces for a stirring rendition of "I Got You, Babe." Look where it got us. Two divorces later, he's a survivalist pamphleteer with a few essential credit cards. I'm still single and fairly normal, and waiting, I guess, for something. Meanwhile, I observe Kenneth, whose latest lover is Blair. For a period before Blair, they were all named Lonnie. I'd meet Kenneth and a Lonnie for lunch. They all looked as if their eyes were permanently focused on a distant shore. In two or three months it would be over.

Blair, unlike any of the others, has moved in with him. She is adjusting well to life with a man twice her age. It's probably not much different than living with Mom and Dad, but there's no Mom to tell Blair to turn down the CD. Blair seems at ease with her life at Kenneth's. They go for drives in the country and buy antique blue bottles. They try new cuisines at home. This week it was a Madras spinach-cheese stew.

"Did the fabric bleed when you washed it?" I couldn't help but ask.

The only thing she doesn't understand, she confides to

ELEMENT 109

me, is why Kenneth named his dog Sam Dash.

"Watergate," I explain. "You know, dirty tricks."

"I haven't heard of them. I like the Talking Heads."

"Funny," I say. She looks bored and doesn't answer, brushing the longer side of her hair with an unconsciously alluring gesture. She does have a way. In another life I might kiss her. She displays her left shoulder with the flair of a waiter exhibiting the catch of the day. Then she looks past me, out to sea, but the sea is a window filled with shell-lacked loaves of bread in autumnal colors.

I try again. "Sam Dash was the Democratic counsel." Perhaps she'll take the initiative to look it up in her *Childcraft Encyclopedia*.

"I thought he chose Dash to make a pun on Spot."

"Maybe he's feeling nostalgic for Morse Code. Kenneth did serve in the army."

"He never told me," she says, listening like a good student.

"He was a medic in Vietnam until he got caught smoking grass by the wrong captain."

"Kenneth? He won't even take an aspirin."

"He was young once too."

"I think he's still very youthful."

Youthful, I think, picturing a graying couple on a pink beach. *Sylvia and Leonard keep their youthful good looks with regular doses of murderous thoughts.*

"I have to go, Blair," I say. "I have an appointment with my chiropractor at eleven. My lumbago's acting up."

"Oh," she says, serious, concerned. Maybe Kenneth loves her because she's so easy to fool. Was I that gullible when Kenneth and I were lovers? Probably, because we almost married before we decided that we canceled each other out. I laughed at all of his jokes before he got to the punch lines, and sometimes I finished his sentences. We agreed on what wasn't funny as well, like the time at the Christmas party when Dr. Keegan, the knee man, sang "Oh, Danny Boy," and wept onto Dr. Lui's lab coat. We became too secure in our perspectives, bitter after a while at having our worst suspicions confirmed daily. Then bored. By the time our relationship ended, our conversations went something like this:

Kenneth: Did you see that Dan looked so—
Marcy: I thought so too. Wasn't it because—
Kenneth: Yes. And did you know—
Marcy: Sure I know. Janie—
Kenneth: Has it all wrong. It was the—
Marcy: For sixteen thousand dollars how can he be so—
Kenneth: Simple. All he had to do—
Marcy: Besides, Dan isn't one to—
Kenneth: I know he likes to—
Marcy: Suffer. He likes to—
Kenneth: Suffer.

In a few years we might have abandoned speech altogether. Public television might have made a documentary on us, along with the man who opens cans by the force of concentration. With Blair there are long hours of briefings, nicely shaped sentences, whole skeins of connections to be unraveled. That is, until Kenneth discovered that Blair understood the Sam Dash allusion.

I received a call at work. I had a deadline to meet. My fourteen inches of type about the best Italian beef on Halsted Street were due in at 3 P.M.

ELEMENT 109

"I have a problem," he sighed. Preceding his sigh was the first full sentence that Kenneth had spoken to me in years. "Blair is growing up."

"She's already six feet tall."

"Intellectually, Marcy. She wanted to discuss Watergate at dinner. She's reading *Blind Ambition* and *All the President's Men*. She disagrees with Woodward and Bernstein about the identity of Deep Throat."

"No!"

"And she's reading my scientific journals. She told *me* all about Element 109." His voice expressed the outrage of a Bluestocking at a brewer's convention.

"Heavy."

"Right. It's the heaviest element on the periodic chart."

"Don't lug any home. Have it delivered."

"She's turned industrious on me. May I see you tonight?"

"I have pudding class. Tonight it's plum pudding."

"Remember what we used to do at ten o'clock?"

Kenneth means the news. Soon he'll be singing tenor with Dr. Keegan, and he's not even Irish. I don't want to encourage his sentimentality, so I say, "No, what?"

"The news," he whispers.

"That's when news was news. Remember Barbara Jordan? She was a baritone." There's a pause, so I say, "Tell me more about Element 109."

"You'll need a new periodic table."

I have one over my breakfast nook. I love the elements with their evocative names like *Xenon*. Not even a sunset over Mount Fuji can top Xenon for beauty. When I need a lift, I string the names together for an instant mantra:

Promethium, Europium, Californium, Thulium, Erbium. It's better than prayer.

"I can't see you, Kenneth."

He sighs. I used to mistake his resignation for pathology, the brave doctor concealing his condition from the woman he loves. Now I'm able to relax when Kenneth gets sad.

"Kenneth, it just wouldn't be . . ."

"I know."

How does he know when I can't imagine how I might have finished my sentence? "I told Blair about Sam Dash. That is, I gave her a clue. I thought of it as a test. Would Blair change her image? I wanted to imagine her at a big oak library table looking studious, if only to feel better myself."

The next morning I go to Warner's Science Outlet, Inc. The warehouse contains three floors of dried ferns, gyroscopes, monkey skulls, and stalagmite kits, all in dimly lit rooms bathed in formaldehyde.

"I want a periodic table with Element 109," I tell the clerk. He's wearing a scientist's smock and has a demented look about him, as if he's inhaled too much ammonia. He's about Blair's age but more solid than she is. Perhaps it's because his legs are short. Does having short legs make one practical and unassuming?

After looking through a black-and-white catalog, he says, "I'm sorry, ma'am. Our periodic tables don't show an Element 109."

Maybe he thinks I made the whole thing up. "It's new. It's the heaviest element." He looks as if he wished I'd go away. "If I come back in a few days, can I pick up a new chart?"

ELEMENT 109

"I'll call the supplier, but sometimes these changes are slow. There are planets beyond Pluto that were discovered years ago, but on the Styrofoam models routinely sold to schools, the planets stop at Pluto."

Duly sobered, I thank him and leave the store.

Tonight I'm supposed to meet Blair for dinner. Her voice was on my answering machine when I came home from pudding class last night. So was Kenneth's. His messages are dots and dashes:

"Call me if . . . oh" —sigh— "forget it." He leaves no name.

I return Blair's call when I think Kenneth will be at his office. What I've forgotten is that Kenneth is a doctor who takes Fridays off.

"Why are you home?"

"Because I don't golf."

"Is Blair home?"

"No, she does ceramics today. Want to come over?"

"Thanks, but I'm at work. Tell Blair I'll meet her at six. She knows where."

When she meets me at Tosca's, Blair resembles the Clay People who lived in caves on the "Flash Gordon" show. Her overalls are covered with gray dust. Her hair is slicked back and her face is ashen. We order a carafe of wine but decide to forgo dinner. I wish there were more women in the movies who drank with style. Whenever I drink seriously, I feel like Humphrey Bogart. I know it would be healthier for me to identify with Olivia de Havilland.

"It's Kenneth, Marcy."

"What do you mean?"

"I'm not in love with him. I can't really talk to him, and I don't know what to do."

"Tell him," I suggest.

"I can't, Marcy. He's so . . ."

"Earnest? I guess it's a habit. Do you want *me* to tell him?" I think I said it with some irony in my voice.

"Would you, Marcy? Oh, thank you. All he does is lecture me. He'll listen to you. Do you think that you can tell him tonight? I have to go back to the studio and fire a piece before the kiln is turned off."

"Okay, Blair," I say, eyes meeting the carafe. I don't want to look at her. I have a feeling that her dusty getup is a ploy, that a twenty-year-old humanities major is waiting outside, holding her change of clothes and a crisp copy of *Anna Karenina*. I wish them well.

"I'll see Kenneth tonight," I tell her, half wondering if I'm crazy. Blair stands up, begins to offer me a handshake, withdraws it and plants a dusty kiss on my cheek. Then she's out the door.

After I've finished my wine, I walk to the corner and wave casually at a cab, which blurs past me. Now my wave becomes an eccentric gesture that combines window-washing with pointing. It works. Johnny Star Cab number 109 pulls over. Turquoise and white, it resembles a police-car illustration from a child's picture dictionary. My cabdriver is elderly and has a shiny head with red fringe speckled white, like orange juice dashed with rock salt.

We drive in silence. My driver is slow and thoughtful. We are always the last to leave the stoplight. Finally, he turns down Fifty-seventh and stops in front of Kenneth's. My stomach clenches when I see his lights are on.

ELEMENT 109

Kenneth is watching the news. I've had twelve glasses of Chianti and notice that I'm speaking in the hurried clip of 1930's movies.

"It's over, Kenneth."

"I know. It's been over for years, Marcy."

"Not us. You and Blair. She wanted me to tell you it's over. That's why she saw me tonight."

Harry Reasoner, America's most trusted newsman, beams at us. Kenneth's big sigh fills the room. Slinking over, Sam Dash rests his bullet head in Kenneth's lap.

"She'll be fine. Will you?"

"Marcy, let's get married."

"Right, Kenneth."

We both laugh.

"They don't have periodic tables with Element 109," I tell him.

Kenneth says nothing.

SIGNS OF DEVOTION

■ ■ ■ ■ ■ ■ ■ ■ ■ While Dave was away and I was asleep, a sniper fired two shots on our block. The next morning a neighbor child found bullets under Carla and Stanley Penn's magnolia. Harmless as snails, they hadn't come close to a house. The police theorize that it was a prankster. I must confess I wasn't that sniper, though I wish I were, as I wipe off the counter, as I slip off my T-shirt, as Jeff entangles me with his sensitive nerves. I mention the sniper because he signals a change in my relationship with Dave. I used to be afraid to go to bed before he was home. For seventeen years, I listened to my tight heartbeat drumming like a toy until I worried Dave through the door. Something terrible might happen that I might have prevented awake.

Jeff is my first lover, Dave's visiting cousin. After Jeff's marriage failed, he decided to make a tour of all the states he's never visited. His old Datsun contains souvenirs for Billy: deerskin Indian moccasins from Nebraska, a doll face made of dried apples from Iowa, and a plastic bust of Abraham Lincoln, mole and all, from Springfield, Illinois. Leonora has taken little Billy back to Hattiesburg, where she'll live with her mother until they can't stand each other. Leonora's a muralist and needs big walls to keep her happy. I don't think she'll find what she needs in Hattiesburg.

Jeff's sitting on the couch reading *The Journal of Psy-*

chomotor Disorders. When he relaxes, he slouches like laundry. When he slouches, he resembles Dave. "Listen to this," he'll say and read me a paragraph on facial tics. He'll exaggerate the details, and if I consent to watch, act them out with precision. I pretend that I'm enthused. It makes things work more smoothly.

Whenever the phone rings, it's my sister Irene, older than me by twelve years, who uses her radar to call at the worst moments.

"Hi, Irene," I say.

"I'll be late again," Dave replies.

"Call when you'll be on time. It'll save your firm money."

Dave's seeing Donna. She's a cost accountant with turquoise contact lenses and a wet smile. She used to come to family gatherings with Glen, who's British. She'd get a lot of attention showing him off.

"Say 'laboratory,'" she'd tell him. "Say 'aluminum.'"

Like a good parrot, he'd do exactly as she asked. When Glen's mom died of emphysema and he returned to Birmingham last fall, Donna stopped visiting us. I thought it was unfair that she should feel unwelcome without Glen, so I called her.

"This is hard to believe," she said. "Dave claimed you knew."

When I finally understood her meaning, I reeled around the kitchen feeling myself diminished to a dark hot stone. For months when people spoke, I wondered how they could see me.

Dave doesn't know that Donna told me. He's so cordial that I've begun to feel relieved when he's away. Dave attends sales meetings in the Amazon, at resorts with pineapple-shaped swimming pools. He brings me lizard-skin bags he buys duty-free at the airport. In rooms furnished with mahogany antiques rowed down the river by natives, Dave sleeps with Donna. I can picture them buried under the covers, the air conditioner tweeting. I wonder if Donna thinks about me anymore. At home Dave and I sleep in tense shifts, bumper cars passing in the night.

The first time Jeff fell asleep on our couch, his mouth was an "O." His hands, folded in front of him like a diver's, were stiller than hands. He looked like Daniel taking a nap ten years ago, or the little boy I saw in the park asleep under a checkered picnic blanket. When Daniel was small, I used to perform this test: I'd raise his hand above his head, then let it drop. It would fit back in place without disturbing his sleep. "He has a pure heart," Irene used to say. Jeff is twenty-nine, too old to seem like a child.

Three days ago, I was sitting on the floor watching Jeff sleep. When he sensed that I was there, he reached over and pulled me on top of him. At first I wondered if he'd done it unconsciously, dreaming that I was Leonora. I thought of those country songs where somebody says the wrong name in bed.

"What time is it?" he asked after he was inside me.

"Dave's away," I said. "Danny's at school till four."

He dug his head into my hair and said, "Jerri, you're terrific."

It was as simple as that.

The phone rings again. This time it's really Irene, who thinks that Jeff's a nice boy. Her own husband Clark left Irene when she was still young. I remember sitting in my mother's house. From the hi-fi in the front room, I could hear Bobby Darin singing "Mack the Knife." Chain-smoking in the kitchen, Irene was telling my mother about Clark. I watched the ash on her cigarette drop onto the green Formica tabletop and thought about Clark's hair. Can elaborately styled hair predict bad character? I considered asking Irene, but she looked too miserable to bother with me. She'd been crying and her eyes were nearly swollen shut. Around them little plateaus of hives had formed.

After Irene left, my mother smoked a rare cigarette. She inhaled as if she wanted to swallow the world. Then she began a cleaning frenzy that culminated in defrosting the refrigerator and throwing out the wedding-cake top she'd been saving for them. Thinking Irene still might want to keep it, I saved it in my room for a few weeks. When I showed it to Irene, she asked me why I was keeping a pile of crumbs on my closet floor.

Irene has worked for years as a secretary to the president of the roofers' union. She attends theater, plays bingo, and talks endlessly to me. She's pieced together a life from others' leftovers: she works for a man whose wife ran off to Scotland with the union treasurer. Her theater companions are widows who call themselves by their husbands' names, Mrs. John Merllman, Mrs. Norman DeBianca. She plays bingo at an old people's home, cheating to make herself lose. Irene has never been wise about capital. My dad called Clark a jack-of-no-trades. When air-conditioning spread, Clark considered refrigeration, but he moved slower than industry. Besides, there was a place for him in Dad's firm. Soon Dad died and Cress Industries was found to be insolvent. Some evidence pointed to Clark's having mishandled the books. After he took off, there were a few letters, and on their third anniversary, a monkey-faced bank made of a coconut with Irene's name etched on it.

Irene gave the bank to Daniel when he was little. He keeps it on his dresser. He's home now, studying in his room with the door bolted. When he was little, he'd tie a rope to the chair to ensure his privacy. Once I opened the door and upset the chair.

"Expecting terrorists?" I asked him.

"I'm expecting my rights," he countered.

How could I argue?

Daniel's thirteen. Tall for his age, blue-eyed, he has Dave's easy charm and icy way of turning it off. Alone in the bedroom, he's singing along to his radio earphones. His voice is high, sweet even in mimicry. He excels in math and science and hangs black-hole posters all over his room where I once hung Natalie Wood. All the books he reads are called *The Blue Andromeda Whistle Gas Function*.

I say good-bye to Irene, knowing she'll remember something later and call back.

"Did you hear anything more about the sniper?" she asks before hanging up.

"It happened because I was asleep."

"I don't get it. Was it one of your crazy students?"

I teach disturbed children. My job demands that I be perfectly literal, steady as concrete. No humor, puns, asides. I finish a joke, lose speed, return to normal gear; they race ahead, overtake me, crash at a curve. Most of the time I give simple orders in an emotionless voice: "Put down that ruler, Tanya. Rulers are for measuring, not for striking other children."

Alex sets fires, but he's careful to choose self-limiting objects. He has burned towels in a washroom, containing them in a sink. Once he set fire to a window shade, burning it down to the loop at the end of the pull, where it stopped, nowhere to spread. The other children I teach are sullen and quiet twelve-year-olds, each with a diagnosis. We're most successful with delinquents like Craig. His minor life of crime is absorbed in building a defense against the biters, the kickers, the glass breakers.

In the morning Dave says hello. I no longer wake up when he gets into bed. Just before the alarm rings, he could walk in, undress and slip under the sheets. I wouldn't know he hadn't slept with me.

"I got in after one. Wouldn't you know that as soon as I open the door the phone rings? It's for Daniel. 'Why are you up so late?' I shout up the stairs to him. 'What's it your business?' he calls down. I count to ten and decide not to kill him. I'll do something useful. I go outside and dig up some holes to plant the new rose bushes, but I feel stupid digging at two in the morning, so I come inside and take a shower. Jeff's up too. He pours me a big glass of milk and we talk about when we were kids. He remembers us playing *The Count of Monte Cristo* in his yard in Spokane. I don't remember reading it, but he says I stood on the porch stairs and acted like the director, telling the smaller kids what to do.

"Say something to Daniel this morning, Jerri. He listens to you."

SIGNS OF DEVOTION

Daniel's asleep when I'm ready to leave. Our garden looks like it hasn't survived a meteor shower. I leave two notes: for Jeff, "Please plant the rose bushes"; for Daniel, "Call Dad at work."

Rays of sun filtering through the leaded glass windows of the Shedd Aquarium intersect at the coral reef in the lobby. I'm in charge of Alex, the pyromaniac. In an aquarium, my job will be easy. I relax as he presses his cheek to the huge convex glass of the coral reef. He shouts in pretend terror when a saw-nosed shark brushes past his face. Following him from room to room, I put my hand on his windbreaker when he allows me. Sometimes he brushes me away with a fly-flicking motion neither of us is supposed to acknowledge.

In a room of smaller tanks, the angelfish seem suspended in water. Only their undulating antennae indicate life. "They're shaped like triangles," I tell Alex, remembering how Daniel liked to distinguish the forms of objects when he was younger. Alex drums his long fingers, nails bitten to the quick, against the glass. The fish aren't bothered.

"They like you," I tell him.

Inside the display a tiny ceramic diver stretches his hand in front of me. He's pointing outside of the tank. Water bubbles from his head. In the next tank two lamprey eels poke their rubbery heads out of a clay cylinder. Alex's laugh is so strong that I'm embarrassed by my own weak silence. Running from display to display, the carpeted floor absorbing his steps, Alex is the only moving object in the room of slow water-breathers. He lunges toward the angelfish, which never move. He darts to the eels, bobbing to their own ungainly rhythm. He shoots out into the hallway to press his face against the reef. Angelfish, eels, reef—that is his path all morning. Back at school Alex hands me a picture he's drawn, two angelfish facing each other, silver with black stripes, perfect triangles.

That evening Daniel stays at a friend's. The daily paper has dropped the sniper story, though the local paper still claims he's at large.

"I wouldn't be surprised if the guy isn't a terrorist," Irene says.

"How do you know it's not a woman?" I reply.

I pour a bath, climb in and lean my head back on the clammy porcelain. In walks Jeff holding two tall gin and tonics on a tray. I nearly laugh to think what men give you.

"I don't drink."

He pours mine into the water. "Bathtub gin," he says. "May I join you?" He's already taken off his shoes. He's unbuttoning his shirt.

"Can I meet you later?" I ask.

This time Jeff's carrying teacups and some generic sandwich cookies I often give Daniel for lunch. I think of a cat I had when we lived in California. Josey used to bring me dead wading birds, egrets and herons, as signs of devotion. I think of telling Jeff about Josey, but knowledge is only a complication.

"It's hard to believe I'll be leaving soon."
"Right."
"Too bad I can't stay."

"Let's not talk," I say, stirring my tea with a cookie. Then we both laugh without really knowing why.

As soon as Jeff leaves, I'll speak to Dave. I'll tell him it doesn't matter what he does with Donna. There's so much trouble in the world that a little more confusion can't hurt. If Dave tells me I'm generous, I'll ask him to leave. If he knows to be quiet, maybe I'll let him stay.

THE RIVER SHANNON

■ ■ ■ ■ ■ ■ ■ ■ ■ Nancy, my newest ex, said, "Vacationing alone's like going to see a Velcro bullfight."

"What do you mean?"

"In a Mexican neighborhood last summer, they wanted to have a bullfight, but they didn't want to kill the bull, so they used swords tipped with Velcro."

I didn't understand how they could get Velcro to stick on a bull, but her main point was why someone should pay for a ruse.

"Nancy," I said, "vacationing alone is the trend of my future. It's a talent I have to cultivate, and I've chosen the most obvious place to do so."

I thought about what she'd said on the plane ride home. I had gone away for a week and everything had happened. The first boy who kissed my daughter won a Nobel Prize in genetics, the mayor died, and I met Fiona.

The man behind me was spanking his son.

"Take off your seat belt," he said to the boy. "You need to learn a thing or two."

I admit it's hard to travel with children, but it's not easy to travel alone either. While I had stood at Niagara Falls taking the usual snapshots, the ground had been shifting below me and a fine mist containing all the events of my past and future had hit me in the face.

I stayed on the Canadian side of the Falls at a place

THE RIVER SHANNON

called the River Shannon. Don't ask me why they call it that. There wasn't one shamrock in sight. It was a modernist creation done in black, gray, aluminum, and mirrors, somber and streamlined as a funeral home in the twenty-first century. The rooms were colorful, though, and I was happy to see no ice machines near my door. I spent a little time watching Canadian television, mostly American reruns, and a lot of time sleeping. Two afternoons I went down to the swimming pool. "Swim at your own risk," the sign said, as if a circular bath could harbor danger. That's as big as it was. No one else came to swim. I wondered if there was something wrong with the water or whether you simply don't swim at Niagara Falls. Maybe the Falls itself makes the idea of water superfluous.

I had covered myself with a big bath towel and was picturing a cartoon child playing in a sandbox in the desert when a man in a uniform said, "Mr. Price, you're wanted on the phone." The third day of my vacation and someone couldn't live without me.

I stood at the front desk watching my arms grow goose bumps while the nice gray carpet soaked up the moisture from my bare feet. It was my daughter on the phone. She sounded as if someone had been chasing her when she told me that Ronald Girtz had won the Nobel Prize.

"Who?"

"Ronald, the boy I used to see in ninth grade. He had a serious overbite? You once, um, saw us kissing in the rec room?"

How could I forget that? My daughter's on her second marriage and from what she tells me about Chuck, it's not going well either. She was a whiz kid in school and now

■ 102

she's a bank teller. I noticed my feet, which were bluish. The hair stopped right at the ankles, as if my skin were a flesh-colored sock. I said, "That's great, Felice. Tell him congratulations."

"I haven't talked to him in twenty years, Dad. I just thought you'd want to know."

"Well, thanks for calling," I told her. I handed the man the phone and he smiled at me. It was an obsequious smile. I wondered if he'd been listening. I wondered if Canadians like Americans.

On my last night at the Falls, I decided to have dinner at Van's. The hotel and restaurant directory had given it three stars. The worst part of being alone is eating, though I've found that if I take along a book or magazine and order lots of wine, I can usually turn it into a pleasant experience. Yesterday at lunch I'd read the third chapter of *Exodus* three times while finishing some Romanian merlot.

When I asked at the desk how to get to Van's, the clerk said I'd need a cab. I told him I'd prefer to walk, and he pointed me in the direction.

I started out on a narrow sidewalk that bordered a highway. Soon it dwindled to some fine gravel and dirt, then ended, so I found myself walking on the shoulder of the road. I could see the big neon V of the sign for Van's flashing green in the distance on the other side of the highway. While I was wondering how I might cross the divider and the median strip, I heard a sound like a wet firecracker behind me. Something exploded and sizzled. There was a squeal of brakes, followed by a powerful shove, and I was thrown forward but not as far as I'd expect a car to toss me.

THE RIVER SHANNON

In one sense it was as simple as that, but in a more immediate way the moment was prolonged so that getting up was a series of fragile connections, like building a model airplane with old glue. Muscle by muscle, I lifted myself into a crawling position. Then I squatted and held myself at the ankles for a long time. I was looking down in my lap and rocking back and forth. I was thinking about random things—Felice and Chuck's Christmas card of a snowman doing a backbend, the taxi meter from the airport registering my fare like a photo negative, kitchen wallpaper radishes in the first house I ever owned—and I was shivering all over even though I was trying to keep still.

"Are you okay?" a woman asked. Her forehead was extremely light, but the rest of her face was blotchy. It was so red that I couldn't stop staring at her cheeks.

"I think I am," I said and stood up slowly, more airplane glue and cautious fitting together of parts. Did my head sit on my neck, my spine on my legs? I looked myself over and saw that both knees of my slacks were ripped out. I could feel that the skin was scraped, but that's about all that was wrong.

"Thank God," the woman shouted, waving long fingers into the darkening sky. She looked so grateful that I thought she might kiss me. "I was thinking about a flow chart in my briefcase when I heard a huge pop. I guess I had a blowout and I veered up onto the shoulder. I never expected someone to be walking there. When I heard you hit the fender, I thought I might have a heart attack. Then the car somehow stopped, and I saw you sitting there."

I heard sirens and thought I should save my impressions of the accident for the police. The woman hovered over me. I noticed that she'd been wearing earrings shaped like big white telephones but had lost one in the excitement.

The policeman was very young. He came charging out of his squad car like a safety about to intercept a pass. "Are you all right, sir?" he asked.

"I believe I am. Just a little scraped on the knees."

"We'll need to file an accident report. Did your vehicle sustain any damage?"

"I don't have a car."

"Why are you on the highway, sir?"

"I was walking to Van's for dinner. I'm staying at the River Shannon and didn't want to take a taxi."

"May I see an ID?"

I showed him my driver's license and my American Express card. He walked back to his squad car studying each in turn.

An ambulance pulled up. The paramedic who got out was a thick-waisted young woman who looked Swedish. She told me she'd like to take my pulse and blood pressure and look at my knees. She had me sit on the cot in the ambulance. After she checked my vital signs, clucking her tongue and taking notes with a little pencil, she took tincture of iodine and swabbed some on each knee through the holes in my pants.

"Too bad you don't have a sewing kit," I joked.

"I hope they're not too hard on you."

"For what?"

"Walking on the highway. We have laws against hitchhiking."

"I was trying to get to Van's for dinner. I'm on vacation."

"Where are you from?"

THE RIVER SHANNON

"Chicago." From the way her face filled with import and her brows strained to meet above her nose, I thought she'd heard about Felice and Ronald Girtz.

"Did you hear that your mayor died?"

"You're kidding. That's too bad."

"He had a heart attack right in his office." The gesture she made with her hand pantomimed life and death.

"It seems like celebrities die whenever I'm out of town."

She was laughing at that when the policeman handed back my ID and read the account of the accident in a flat voice. He made the whole event sound so mundane that I felt offended, but I wasn't going to argue with his tone. I shook my head in assent, and he told me I was free to go.

"Can I drive you somewhere?" the paramedic asked.

"How about my motel?"

Her name was Fiona but she wasn't Irish. Her parents just wanted to be different. She was twenty-four and had been a paramedic for two years. I told her it must be exciting.

"Only if you like to see people die," she said. "Why don't you change clothes, and I'll come by after work?" She was holding the back of my wrist and stroking it as if I were her patient and she was looking for a good vein.

Fiona had beautiful eyes. When I picture us sitting in my hotel room, that's what I see, eyes like black olives. I was telling Fiona that it's unusual to see someone with light hair and such dark eyes when suddenly she was crying.

"What's wrong?" I asked. She was fiddling with my digital travel alarm. Her upper lip quivered, and her eyes searched the ceiling, for what I don't know.

"My dad," she said.

I wondered if Felice ever cried about me at intimate moments. "What happened?" I asked, placing a commiserating arm around her shoulder.

"I think about him all the time. He lives in South Africa."

"Is he sick?"

"He's as healthy as a horse."

"Well, what's wrong, then?"

"He's an apologist. He writes me letters and tells jokes about the place. Last week some Russian officials visited for the first time since 1956 and the headlines said, 'Reds in Our Beds.'"

"So?"

"How can he live there and be well-adjusted?"

"Maybe he has to be. Why are you thinking about him now anyway?"

When she didn't answer, I put on my reading glasses and opened my book. I thought I'd do something useful.

"Why are you reading?" She closed *Exodus* on chapter 4, and slammed it down on the nightstand. She unhooked my glasses and placed them beside the book. Taking my chin in her hand, she kissed me.

"Do you know how to do CPR?" I asked her.

"Sure thing," she said, turning off the lamp. She rubbed her palms together. They made a papery sound. Then she flexed her muscles and started to massage my chest. I closed my eyes and thought about Felice. I wondered if Chuck knows how to make her happy in the right way.

SIX-OH

■ ■ ■ ■ ■ ■ ■ ■ ■ "Marry a monkey later in life," Lillian read out loud. "Avoid the dog."

"I hope we're avoiding the dog right now." Carl pretended to hold his egg roll up to a magnifying glass.

"I'm reading my place mat, Carl, not commenting on lunch."

"I was thinking of going on the Oprah Winfrey diet," Carl said, pinching his midriff.

"I tried the Richard Simmons diet years ago. I can't say I was too impressed. You had to suffer. Besides, Oprah's diet's for people who need to lose half of themselves. You know that chef in New Orleans?"

"Paul Prudhomme?"

"Right. He could use her diet." Lillian smoothed her hair and patted the bodice of her dress. It was a gesture she always used when she had finished speaking.

Carl guessed that Lillian had once been shy and still checked to see if speaking had disheveled her. He watched her arms ripple in her short-sleeved dress and her silver bracelet depicting the Hawaiian Islands clank against a teacup. He didn't understand why he found her so entertaining at lunch. At the accounting office, she was a terror. Maybe Julius Caesar had merely been difficult in the Senate.

Lillian reapplied her lipstick in the blade of her butter knife. She saw Carl watching her. "Before I worked for Mr.

SIX-OH

Dickey, I was a waitress. I learned to do this years ago." She smiled, revealing lipstick over the lipline. "Before I was born, Clara Bow's mouth became the standard. Sweetheart lips." She tossed Carl a demure kiss.

He pretended to catch it. "Isn't it your birthday soon?"

"The big six-oh."

"You don't look a day over fifty-nine."

"I keep worrying that they'll find me dead and use one of those captions under my corpse on TV, 'sixty-year-old bookkeeper.' Doesn't sound too appetizing."

"It could be worse. It could say 'sixty-year-old virgin.'"

"I don't have to impress you with my exploits, dear. I'm old enough to be your grandmother. Show some respect."

"I do, Lillian," Carl said, taking the check from her hand.

"You must be drunk if you're offering to pay. You know what they call you at work? Carl McScrooge."

Carl feigned amazement.

"Why do you think they don't ask you to contribute to the special-occasions committee of the real estate division anymore?"

"Because there's nothing too special about a bunch of ladies having their gall bladders out."

"I had my gall bladder out."

"That's different. I'd have gladly contributed to you. It's just that I object to blanket charity. One's participation should be discretionary."

"You can't speak for ten seconds without showing off your vocabulary. No wonder you don't get along with people your age."

"People my age don't understand me." Carl took the napkin from the empty place setting and pretended to weep.

"There, there," Lillian said, patting his wrist. "Let's get back to the office before the rumor mill starts churning."

Carl stood in the front room. He hoped the man across from him, the one he'd seen doing amazing shadow aerobics, was watching. That was the charm of old courtyard buildings. They brought out the best in shy people. Every night at eleven he stood in the same triangle of light and undressed. Even if the man wasn't interested, he'd eventually have to notice Carl. If not that man, there were six other windows from which someone could observe him.

Before he went to bed, he read another chapter of the book on savants that Lillian had given him. He propped it up on his stomach and read one word at a time. He liked reading slowly before bed, becoming aware of the sounds of letters as sleep overtook him and he dropped off. He read a fact that amazed him, that savants don't so much have good memories as they aren't able to forget. He recalled a term from college English, "negative capability," and wondered if it had anything to do with the sentence he'd read. What would it be like to remember every sensation he'd experienced? It might lead to premature aging to be responsible for so much of one's past. He did wish he could remember a few things more accurately. Gavin's face, for instance, was receding from him. His brown eyes were simply gone. Why could he remember every crack and crag of Lillian's chin and not be able to see Gavin's nose anymore? He had a photo somewhere, but that was beside the point, and he was too tired to look for it. He closed his eyes and saw the house in the country where he'd met Gavin. The stairs were made of red brick. The sun was low in the sky. A carpet of bugs hovered over the pond near the barn where his uncle stored tools and a snowmobile.

On Lillian's sixtieth birthday, Carl promised to obey her wish for a quiet evening. That meant seizing the plans for the celebration from the hands of Sheila Vincent, a secretary who looked like the young Barbara McNair, and was in charge of the special-occasions committee. That morning on the way to work, Carl had been thinking of changing his name. It was so guttural, so old-fashioned. What were his parents thinking he'd amount to with a name like his? People spit it out of their mouths like phlegm. "Carl, Carl, Carl," he said as the el train roared through the tunnel.

He should have been less abrupt, but it just came out in a flurry when he saw Sheila Vincent in line for a doughnut downstairs. "Whatever you're planning for Lillian's birthday, she won't like it."

"And who are you," Sheila asked, opening her eyes wide and articulating each word like she was making a political speech, "her lady-in-waiting?"

"Lillian told me to tell you people that she wants no party. She thinks that sixty should be a solemn occasion."

"If I didn't know you'd run and tell Lillian, I'd express my true feelings. As it is, let me speak in my official capacity. I wish to inform you and the Sea-Hag that we're merely planning to have cake, coffee, and a gift at work. I couldn't find enough employees to attend a social function for Lillian, unless, of course, it were a wake."

Carl turned on his heels and took the elevator to eighteen. It was better this way. They'd go to dinner somewhere special and maybe see a play or hear music. He'd buy her a corsage.

"It was hard, but I convinced them, Lillian. They agreed to have cake and coffee at the office and leave us alone to our fantasies the night in question."

"Who did you talk to, Sheila?"

"None other than Ms. Sheet Cake of 1987."

"I hope she wasn't too disappointed."

"She took it like a woman."

After dinner on Lillian's birthday, Carl planned to take her to My Brother's Keeper to hear a gay folksinger named Earl Shilott. Although they had never spoken about it, he was sure that Lillian knew he was gay, especially if Sheila Vincent, with her limited capacity, could guess. Lillian never asked him if he was seeing girls, as his mother still did when he called her in Cleveland Heights.

"Met any good-looking girls in Chicago?"

"Ouch! That's one right now, tearing out strands of my hair. Excuse me for a minute, Mom. 'Judy, put my shoe back where you found it! Get your hands off my shaving mug! I'll give you a souvenir at the door.'"

"Can't you be serious for a minute, Carl?" his mother asked, but he could hear her amusement in the way she said his name.

He'd hardly spoken to his father since the summer before last. They had been riding in a golf cart at his father's country club when Carl had simply said, "You know about me, Dad, right?"

His father had pretended not to hear, and then they were at the next green. Carl had felt the adrenaline drain out of his fingers and had never mentioned it again. Surely Uncle Dan knew, from the way Carl and Gavin had carried on

SIX-OH

that weekend in the country. Looking back, though, Carl realized that he had been more discreet than he'd planned. He was less so with his mother on the phone or with Lillian at lunch, but he was only truly outrageous at home. Just last night standing in the window, he had taken his penis in his hand. He knew he could get arrested, but it was his own apartment, after all, and nobody had to look. Let them draw their damn draperies rather than see him double over with pleasure and effort.

Carl didn't know Earl Shilott, but he'd seen him perform a few times and had made important eye contact with him the last time he was at the bar. Shilott was a lot older than Carl, perhaps fifty, and not as handsome as impressive. He was heavyset and barrel-chested, which made him look shorter standing up than he appeared to be sitting down. He had wavy hair that he combed straight back and small features for such a big man. Carl imagined he would look better dressed than naked. Shilott had recorded a few albums but was a well-kept secret from the general public. Carl wondered if he minded how limited his audience was. If he did mind, he could have changed a few pronouns and ended up with entirely different songs. Carl had read on a record jacket that Earl had been a forest ranger and a merchant marine. It was a definite liability for Carl to work in accounting. He'd change his profession to something more exotic. Maybe Greenpeace needed a good internal auditor. Then when someone at a bar asked what he did, he could say he saved whales, instead of changing the subject.

An hour before he was supposed to pick up Lillian, the phone rang. He was taking her orchid corsage out of the refrigerator and putting it with his coat so he wouldn't forget it when he left.

"It's me, Carl," Lillian said. "If you don't think it's all right, I want you to tell me. Okay?"

"How can I say okay before I know what it is?"

"Well, listen then. Vance just dropped in. He used to be the doorman at our building. He wanted to drop over and give me a surprise for my birthday. I suggested that he join us for the evening, but if you don't think so, he'll understand."

Carl was outraged, but he put on his most pleasant voice. "Whatever will make you happy, Lillian. It's your six-oh."

"So you'll pick us up at the same time?"

"Seven. Did you tell Vance about the music later?"

"He thinks that'll be fine."

"Okay then; see you in an hour."

No wonder nobody likes her, Carl thought when he got off the phone. Making a commotion about her quiet birthday until someone better knocks on her door. What was this, an Ivan Albright honeymoon for Lillian and her doorman, with Carl as porter, *maître d'*, and the sucker who'd pick up their check?

He took the corsage out of the box and shredded it into the garbage disposal. Then he turned it on for a minute and listened to it ingest the orchids. The bow would get caught in the mechanism and he'd have to dig it out later. Meanwhile, he felt better. He looked at himself in the mirror on the way out, pulled his hand through the hair he kept longer on top and short on the sides, put on his black overcoat, and waved good-bye to himself.

The car was parked a block away on Kenmore. He began walking and heard footsteps behind him. Two young women made a wide U onto the grass to avoid him as they passed. They were convulsed in laughter.

"That's him for sure!" the shorter one gasped to her companion.

Carl blanched to think they'd been his audience all those evenings. Overcome with embarrassment, he collapsed into his car. Maybe he'd have to move out. He could always go back to Cleveland, where he had better friends than Lillian, or to New York, where no one knew him. Uncle Dan would have him for the summer. Dan liked it when Carl was around, if only because he was afraid to be alone in the country now that Aunt Lottie was dead. Carl and Dan could take long drives through the Connecticut mountains and go into town for little things like nails and drill bits. Carl loved hardware stores, with their metallic hum and impersonal smell. And Uncle Dan was at least interesting to talk to. He'd had a life, unlike most people he knew. Dan could show him the photos he'd taken in Kenya and the Philippines and Liberia. Dan understood him better than Lillian did, that was for sure.

He had ten minutes before he was supposed to pick up Lillian and Vance, but he needed to buy a new corsage. The little Korean flower store on Broadway was just closing. He ran in and asked for a corsage.

"All out," the owner said, looking at the clock.

"Can you make one?"

"Ten dollar."

"Fine."

He thought he'd fall asleep on his feet before the man twirled the last bow around the bent metal stem. When the man began to wrap it as a gift, Carl looked at his watch. He was already five minutes late.

"No bow, no bow!" He placed his money on the counter.

"Ten fifty-seven," the owner shouted before Carl reached the door.

He pulled a dollar out of his wallet, crumpled it into a ball, and threw it toward the man.

"That was lovely," Lillian said, wiping some whipped cream off her cheek. Flowers and champagne and strawberry shortcake."

"Don't slight the main course," Vance said.

Vance wasn't that bad. He was a little older than Carl would have liked and not exactly suave, but there was some innate charm about him. He was very kind to Lillian and interested in what Carl had to say. He was impressed that Carl was an accountant and asked the kind of questions about Carl's work that meant he was listening closely. He followed Carl with serious eyes and tried to include Lillian as well. When Carl asked Vance what he did, he wasn't embarrassed to say he cleaned apartments so that he could set his own hours and make a good salary working half-days.

"A good salary!" Lillian said. "His apartment looks like a raja's. Leather this and leather that, and you should see his coffee table."

When Vance didn't offer to describe his coffee table, Carl said, "Well, what about it, Vance?"

"Black marble. It's very unusual. I bought it in Milan."

"See, he travels too. Carl thinks you have to go to college in the East to lead a refined life."

SIX-OH

"I'm not a snob, Lillian." Turning to Vance, he said, "How can someone from Cleveland be a snob?"

"That's where they're usually from," Lillian said.

"Because it's your birthday, Carl will allow that one to pass," Vance said and grinned at them both.

It occurred to Carl that Vance resembled a younger Lawrence Welk if Lawrence Welk were a redhead with black glasses.

"So Lillian tells me we're going to see Earl Shilott."

"Have you seen him?"

"I know Earl. You get to meet a lot of people in the doorman trade. Earl had a friend who lived in Lillian's building a while back. He'd come to see his friend now and then."

"Did you know him socially?"

"No, we just talked when he'd visit this man. You remember Mark Penney, don't you, Lillian?"

"Didn't he move away?"

"Yes," Vance said.

"And then?" Carl asked. He was becoming annoyed at Vance's reticence.

"There is no *and then*. After he moved away, I didn't see him or Earl anymore."

They rode in silence to My Brother's Keeper. By the time they had arrived, Earl Shilott had finished his first set, and there were no seats at the side tables near the stage.

"Looks like we'll have to stand for now," Carl said.

"Carl, I'm exhausted. Standing doesn't sound like much fun for an old lady like me. Why don't I get a cab and you two stay on?"

Carl was perfectly happy to accept Lillian's offer but

SIGNS OF DEVOTION

Vance said, "We can't desert the birthday girl. Why not come back to my place for some brandy? I'll play Earl's album, and Carl won't miss a thing."

"If it's fine with Carl, it's fine with me." Lillian shrugged.

"Okay," Carl said. He saw the back of Earl's head but couldn't see the rest of him from where they were standing. He'd sound ungracious if he insisted on staying, but he lingered behind long enough to emphasize to Vance and Lillian that it hadn't been his idea to leave.

When they reached Vance's building, just two doors away from Lillian's, Lillian said, "You know, I'm going to sound like a party-pooper, but the champagne has gone straight to my head and I need to lie down. You two can get along without me, no?"

"Just one drink?" Vance asked.

"I won't be responsible for the damage at this point," Lillian said and pretended to pass out.

Carl dropped her in front of her building. Vance walked her in and spent a few minutes talking to the current doorman, an elderly Jamaican.

Back in the car, Vance occupied the front seat Lillian had vacated. "To my place, then?"

"Whatever." Carl felt warm and nervous. "Did Lillian set this up?"

"What do you mean?"

"Did you just happen to stop by around six?"

"No, she invited me for dinner. We're old friends, you know."

"Are all of Lillian's friends like us?"

"What do you mean?"

"I mean does she have any women friends?"

SIX-OH

"Not that I know of."

"Does she have many gay friends?"

"Not that I know of."

"We're her only two friends?"

"Quite possibly. Plus a sister she sees on holidays."

"You were her only friend before I began working at her office?"

"Exactly, but we can't sit here all night, you know."

Carl started driving toward Vance's, but he had no enthusiasm for finishing the evening as Lillian had ordained. He guessed it was nice of her to think of him, but he couldn't go through with it.

"Can we get together some other time?" Carl asked Vance.

"That would be fine, Carl, if you want to make this an early evening." Vance gave Carl one of his cards. It said, "Mr. Clean. Vance Erdray. 555-2241."

"How was Lillian's birthday bash? Did you two have a cozy time?" Sheila asked.

"It was very nice." Carl pushed past her off the elevator.

Lillian's desk was behind a special partition toward the back of the office. He imagined that she had sat there for forty years in the same position, inhaling her cigarettes and balancing the books that Mr. Dickey kept on his two smaller enterprises. Lillian was the only employee without a computer. Her part of the office was like an accounting museum.

"Top of the morning," Lillian said, looking up from her adding machine. She patted her forehead and winced. "How did it go last night?"

"How did what go?"

"You and Vance. He's a nice boy, isn't he?"

"He's not a boy any more than you're a girl. He's a man, and for your information, it didn't go."

"Was something wrong?"

"You were wrong, Lillian. Why did you think I'd appreciate meeting Vance?"

"You're new in the city. I thought he might introduce you to some people, you know, show you around."

"I'll thank you to stay out of it, Lillian."

She imitated his annoyed voice. He walked away.

"Ready for lunch?" she said at eleven thirty. "All I want is some toast."

"I have too much to do." Computer printouts were unfurled all over his desk. "Maybe tomorrow, Lillian," he said, guessing that she wouldn't ask again if he refused.

That night Carl pulled down his shades and undressed in the bathroom. He was thinking of calling Uncle Dan and asking him about the prospects for summer when the phone rang.

"It's Vance. I was wondering if I might drop by. I have something I thought you'd be interested in seeing."

"It's kind of late," Carl said.

"It doesn't have to be right now. It can be tomorrow or the next day."

"Well, I'm awake. You might as well bring it over now."

Twenty minutes later Vance was standing in Carl's front room with a bag in his hand. Carl hadn't asked him to sit down or taken his coat. Carl had gotten dressed again and thrown his dirty clothes, unfolded laundry, and dishes behind the door that separated his front room from the efficiency kitchen.

"Nice place you have."

"Sure," Carl said. "It's temporary."

"I have an old album that Earl Shilott made. Want to hear it?"

Carl pointed to the stereo and stared at the jacket cover. It must have been from the sixties. Earl Shilott was young and much thinner. He wore a Nehru jacket. He had been a member of a rock group called The Abacus.

Vance sat on Carl's one chair while Carl took up most of the couch.

"Most of it is instrumental, but Earl's voice is unmistakable." When Earl began singing, Vance pointed his finger in the air. "Hear him?"

Carl listened as Earl sang about missing a girl who rode a horse over a cliff. "I can't believe he'd sing that."

"But his voice. How do you like his voice?"

"I don't much care for it. I like his songs now. His voice was never great. That's why he's stuck at that bar forever."

"Sorry," Vance said. "I thought you'd like it."

"I do. Thanks. I guess I'm just too opinionated."

Vance took off the record and sat next to Carl on the couch. His hand was near Carl's shoulder. "Would you like me to introduce you to Earl?"

"Not really."

Carl wished Vance would go away. He closed his eyes and tried to think of Gavin's face. He saw his Uncle Dan and the Korean florist. He saw his father and their old neighbors, the Igoes. Then he saw Gavin clearly. He opened his eyes and smiled in appreciation.

SIGNS OF DEVOTION

Vance's face was over his. Taking off his glasses, Vance kissed him. Carl didn't fight it, but he didn't kiss back either. As soon as Vance was through with him, he'd call Uncle Dan and make summer plans. Maybe if he got all the details right, Gavin would sit with him on the red stairs and watch the sun disappear behind the hills.

"Want to go to bed?" Vance was asking.

"I have to make a phone call." Carl thought it was the most stupid piece of truth he could have whispered.

SOMEWHERE NEAR TUCSON

■ ■ ■ ■ ■ ■ ■ ■ ■ There are pictures of Barbara's grandfather looking French: beret and cane, straw hat, awning-striped blazer. No lowly Morris from the provinces of Hungary: an American Frenchman who couldn't speak French, barely English; who drank Jack Daniels and smoked Havana cigars; who cheated on his wife; who was a hairdresser to the stars. Barbara would have liked to have asked him what it was like to cut Clark Gable's hair, but before she knew him very well, he'd disappeared. There were a few postcards from Greece, but they were thrown away. You weren't supposed to leave a wife of forty-two years and take the entire savings account.

Barbara's first plane trip was to Los Angeles. Her mother wore a beige linen suit and the kind of pillbox hat that Jackie Kennedy had made popular. Her legs were thin, long, and shapeless like folded draperies. A cigarette hung out of her mouth. As soon as the plane got off the ground, her mother lit up. Barbara charted their place in the sky by the number of cigarettes she smoked. Three got them from Illinois to Iowa; Nebraska took six. Before she dozed off, she calculated that fourteen more would get them to Los Angeles.

For a week Barbara watched her mother console her grandmother. They took walks along Venice Beach and held hands like sweethearts. Sometimes Barbara and Martha followed them along, walking in their shadows, kicking sand at each other, occasionally resting on benches to give the two women privacy. When late afternoon came, mothers and daughters would sit on folding lawn chairs outside the basement apartment their grandmother had taken to economize. Martha would braid Barbara's long hair and make oaths: that she'd kill her grandfather if she ever saw him again, that she'd never marry a man. Barbara would drift, picturing the beach in Greece where water from the Aegean lapped over his hairy legs. She wondered if he'd brought his straw hat along and whether the new unsmiling lady, whose photo her grandmother kept stacked with the bills on the kitchen table, would like such a hat.

After the apartment cooled off in the evening, Barbara's mother and grandmother would cook dinner in unison, feed the girls silently, and tell them to go to bed. Barbara and Martha took turns on a scratchy embossed couch the color of dirty heather. Mother and Grandmother shared a blond double bed that Morris had once snored in. They'd whisper longer than Barbara could strain to stay awake. Sometimes she heard long sobs and words like "bastard." She imagined them twisting her grandmother's benign face. Just before Barbara would fall asleep, she'd picture a photo she'd seen in *Life* magazine. Picasso was smiling, at peace with the world. Many women like her grandmother were crying for him even as he posed for the camera.

Barbara's parents had twin beds, and they certainly didn't make love. They fought once a month when her mother balanced the checkbook. Every two weeks she'd see her father stroke her mother's passing breast, usually in the

SIGNS OF DEVOTION

kitchen after dinner. Helen would say, "Oh-Dan!" as if they were connected syllables. Helen's response was definite enough, but Barbara never understood what it indicated. The needle hovered between gratitude and disgust, giving Barbara too much room for interpretation. She couldn't understand how both feelings could coexist in one mother.

In the top drawer of her father's dresser, along with his monogrammed handkerchiefs and silver cuff links, were his Navy-issue before-and-after photos of Nagasaki. Before the bombing there had been trees and houses. After it, there was rubble heaped on rubble. Strangely, both photos were devoid of people. Because the photos smelled like her father, there was a troubling intimacy about them. She would have tossed them out, but then he'd have known she'd been snooping. Underneath the photos she found the pack of Trojans. As she read the instructions and realized what they were, her heart bumped along like a dump truck. Why would he have hidden them there? He must have meant to keep them a secret from Helen.

Based on her discovery, Barbara concocted a wild sex life for her father, evenings at the Alibi Inn on Lincoln Avenue with his graying secretary Astrid, whose name Barbara remembered by picturing the six-pointed star over the 8-key on her typewriter. It was thrilling to imagine that her father loved Astrid, who wore a hearing aid. Maybe the hearing aid was a ploy. Who would be suspicious of a nearly deaf secretary? Not Helen, whose interests ran more to crossword puzzles and medical lexicons, which she read for entertainment. "Read this," she'd say to Barbara, handing her the definition of "petit mal." Would Helen have cared that

SOMEWHERE NEAR TUCSON

Dan and Astrid were on the blue carpet of his office, her little pearl eyeglass string tangled near her pursed waiting lips, Dan vibrating above her like a helicopter? Astrid had short legs and too little chin, but Dan was soft and round and couldn't have complained.

On the day that Barbara married Roger, she thought of asking her mother about Astrid. Now that they were equals, women, they could share the devastating knowledge. They were standing in the fluorescent aqua-and-pink washroom of the Palmer House Hotel. The light made Helen's fern-and-orchid corsage already look limp. Barbara felt like a potted palm in her wedding gown. Weren't brides supposed to look radiant? She was giving off humidity like a rain forest. Beads of sweat collected on her forehead underneath the sequined veil.

"Whatever happened to Astrid?" Barbara asked.

"I think she died in retirement somewhere near Tucson," Helen answered, smacking her lips at the mirror to blot the lipstick.

"Was she deaf?"

"I don't remember."

"Didn't she wear a hearing aid?"

"Maybe."

"Then she must have been deaf."

By then the thick opening strains of Bach had leaked through the air shafts, and it was time for Barbara to walk down the aisle. In a teary pre-marital confession, she had already told Roger of her suspicions about Astrid and Dan. Roger blamed the entire incident on nerves and didn't seem very interested except in Astrid's pearl eyeglass chain. He'd smiled at that detail, recalling a music teacher in grade school who'd worn the same model.

Thinking of Astrid dead in retirement, Barbara repeated her vows listlessly. She watched her parents sitting together in the first row of chairs, small and wrinkled, constrained by their formal clothes, abject in their joy.

Martha was eighteen the summer she and Marc went into her bedroom and closed the door. They didn't lock it. So blatant an exclusion would have provoked Barbara's anger and tears. With the door unlocked, Barbara could theoretically join them, but she never dared to turn the knob. Instead, she spent most of her Saturday evenings alone watching "Hootenanny." Sometimes she wondered if Jack Linkletter really liked women, or if Paul Stookey ever slept with Mary Travers, whose mouth was so wide and intelligent. And why was it that Barbara didn't know Peter's last name? Surely he had one. And who did he sleep with when Paul and Mary were together?

When the Christy Minstrels were introduced, Barbara took a flying leap off the pastel-green plastic-covered love seat and headed for Martha's door. She heard giggling and saw them in her mind, Martha seductively unhooking her padded bra and Marc caressing every spit curl on her forehead. Barbara pretended that her momentum couldn't be checked and hurled her body into the room. She landed on the center of the leopard jigsaw puzzle that Martha and Marc were demurely piecing together on the linoleum, greeting their questioning faces with an exaggerated smile.

SOMEWHERE NEAR TUCSON

About the same time Barbara and her friend Rhoda practiced making out. Usually Barbara would be the boy. That meant lying atop Rhoda (young missionaries) and planting kisses on her small twelve-year-old lips. Later Rhoda became a nutritionist, and her brother Cary, who had sometimes watched, drowned while on downers the summer he was twenty. At the funeral Barbara stood to the side, feeling responsible for Rhoda's destiny. Rhoda had grown up thin and wary. Men were probably afraid to touch her. Even in Geneva, Switzerland, where she worked for the World Health Organization, there were military attachés who made wide circles around Rhoda.

One night while Marc was on vacation with his parents at Niagara Falls, Martha showed Barbara how to French-kiss. She demonstrated it on the back of Barbara's wrist, where the skin was softest. Martha also performed the swooping kiss, which she said was very European, by draping Barbara over her bent elbow. Twelve years later, when Barbara was a graduate assistant and a history professor from Amsterdam caressed her in an empty lecture hall, it was the swooping kiss she superimposed on the scene.

"It was so stupid," Barbara later told Roger when summing up the experience. "Imagine kissing me where a student might have seen."

Knowing that Barbara's stories had to be met with polite interest bordering on wonder, Roger leered with feigned lust. "Good thing you weren't horses," he added.

"What do you mean?"

Roger, having grown up on a farm, held the upper hand in nature lore. "Horses scream like people when they're having sex. He'd never have gotten away with it if you'd been horses."

Barbara's favorite story was about Eric, her eighth-grade boyfriend, though boyfriend wasn't precisely right, since Barbara shared Eric with Peggy, her best friend. It was Peggy who wore his portrait inside her heart-shaped locket, and who, they agreed, would marry him one day. Meanwhile, since Peggy would be at an Irish folk-dancing convention, Barbara could ask Eric to the eighth-grade graduation party, a boat ride on the *Wendella* along Chicago's lakefront. What were the parents thinking kids would do on a dark boat late in June, lights from shore bobbing like needles in the water? It would be the last time that many of them would see each other. Some were moving away. Others, like Eric, were off to private high schools on their way to careers in military intelligence. Of course, they'd feel compelled to say good-bye in bold cinematic gestures, passionately as Tony and Maria or Lieutenant Cable and Bloody Mary's daughter.

Barbara was wearing a seersucker shirt with an enlarged zipper that opened to her navel, so popular that summer of Mod clothing. One hundred feet from shore, Eric kissed her. He touched her breasts through cloth and bra as Barbara mentally rehearsed, "Oh-Eric!" then spoke it without ambiguity.

"We were never really friends," she whispered.

"I'm sorry," he said and bowed his head.

The rest of the evening was an apology that made for Barbara a natural pairing of love and regret. One bounced into her feelings with the other in tow, like a speed boat and a water-skier.

Eric became a high school swimming champ. Barbara and Peggy drifted apart, though Barbara missed Peggy's sauna and her parents' exotic Long Island accents.

Twice a week Barbara and Roger go to a restaurant ostensibly to eat, but their real purpose is to thrash out a point of argument. All week the tension wells up until it spills over into the gyros or mulligatawny or masala dosa.

"You're impersonal," she says.

"What?" Roger asks, wondering how many arguments a week the patient Guatemalan waiter hears.

"Nothing."

"Did you say I'm impersonal?"

"Let's not discuss it." Barbara focuses her eyes on a light equidistant between the ceiling fan and a slate announcing the catch of the day.

"Okay, we won't discuss it."

"Well, you are," Barbara prods.

"Are what?"

"Discussing it."

Barbara is distracted by a woman at the next table telling her companion, "You always bring me gifts that are dead!"

She surveys their table for evidence but sees only margarita glasses, guacamole, and chips with salsa. Barbara pictures the man in a pet store, aquariums swarming with skeletal fish. Then she hears the woman say, "Stop giving me your sick plants!"

Barbara shares an amused look with Roger. She wonders who will spread this story first among their friends.

SIGNS OF DEVOTION

The next day Barbara is waiting for Roger to pick her up at school. She has signs of a head cold, and hopes that the Joseph Cornell show at the Art Institute will rev up her depleted curiosity.

Standing near her is a dignified Indian man, who might be a fellow faculty member. He is wearing a camel-hair coat, a white crew-neck sweater, and gray-and-black houndstooth slacks. The slacks are slightly long so that they spill over the toes of his shoes, looking salt-stained and defeated.

The man is speaking. At first Barbara doesn't understand that he's speaking to her. She sees him pointing, but before she connects his voice with his gestures, he has removed a man's shoe, cut out to resemble a woman's sandal, and is pointing at his toes.

"Aren't they beautiful?"

"Beautiful?" Barbara asks dreamily.

"My toes. I think that they are beautiful." He is wiggling pink polished toenails under a nylon stocking.

"They're very nice," Barbara replies and looks down, down, down.

At the Cornell show she feels bored and distant. She can't concentrate on the boxed owls and children's blocks or naive collages suggesting false age. She remembers an exhibit she saw in Paris of the little dolls and chess pieces of the murdered Dauphin. She can see them as clearly as the boxes in front of her.

On the way back to the car, Barbara tells Roger about the Indian man and his toes.

"You have radar for those types," Roger smiles. "They must know how interested you are in theories of love."

• • •

SOMEWHERE NEAR TUCSON

Later that evening Barbara is shaving her legs in the bathtub and thinking about a dinner party when her grandparents were still together. At the same time that her grandfather seemed to be giving her grandmother an admiring glance, Barbara noticed a large white brooch perched asymmetrically on the black bodice of her grandmother's dress. She watched it moving slowly down the slope of her grandmother's breasts as she breathed. She realized it wasn't a piece of jewelry. It was a fish bone making its way to her lap.

WHERE EVENTS MAY LEAD

■ ■ ■ ■ ■ ■ ■ ■ ■ Frederick uses his summer vacations in the way that other people use alcohol, cocaine, religious retreats, class reunions, warrior weekends. Fifty weeks of the year, he is the husband of Elizabeth, who's kept her maiden name, Griffon, and the father of Amy Griffon-Tandy and little Jonah Griffon-Tandy. But two weeks every summer, while Elizabeth goes to a resort with an innovative camp program for the children, Frederick goes off alone to see what he is like. Some summers he agrees with the world's assessment of him that he is dull, the summer he took the tour of Vermont's covered bridges, for instance. Another summer he shot the rapids of more than one petulant river and came back to try his cases with a new deep register in his voice. Frederick likes the way the world, clear as a glass window, ignores him this morning while he sits at the harbor near the ferry landing, one of many tourists in colorful cotton shirts who've just invaded Vinalhaven, Maine. To escape the feeling of being part of the mob, he's lagged behind while the other passengers are reclaiming their cars or taking to foot. In the distance, he can see a row of white frame buildings that must be his eventual destination.

"The harbor's crowded today." Frederick looks up and sees a girl whose face is simple and shiny. "Lots of tourists."

"I'm a tourist," he says, slightly embarrassed, admitting

that he's sought out a place the locals may think ordinary. It's like discovering that your wife, viewed at a distance at a noisy office party, isn't as pretty or assured as you had once believed.

"Where ya from?"

"New York."

"You live right in the city?"

"Across from Central Park." Should he tell her that he is a district attorney, or won't she care? He notices that the girl eyes him sideways and always breaks contact when she speaks. She has a good profile, though her nose is a little short, making her what one would call cute rather than pretty. She wears a blue-striped tank suit and cutoffs. Her bones are delicate and her breasts small. She is barefoot, but around her right ankle is a bracelet, as was the fashion when Frederick was her age twenty years ago. If he squints down, he can almost read the name, Lois or Louise. Restrained by a black ribbon, her hair is luxurious. The color of apricots, it flares in a pool at her meager, thin neck.

"I'm a district attorney," he adds. What harm can it do?

"You mean you arrest people?"

"No, I just convict them when I'm lucky. My name is Fred."

"Like Flintstone?

"Like Frederick," he blushes.

"I'm Dolores."

He feels confused. Why is she wearing an ankle bracelet saying Lois? Has he read the name wrong? He'd put on his glasses, but they make him self-conscious. He takes a longing look at the bay, where lobster boats filled with weather-beaten traps are bobbing out of focus in the high water. Maybe the inscription says Louis. Maybe she's going steady.

"Are you here for the summer?" Frederick asks.

"We're natives. My mother's a schoolteacher, and my father runs the business at Shears." Dolores points to an adjacent concrete-slab building, whose yellow-and-blue sign displays the profile of two Neanderthals in need of grooming. "Heard of Carver's?"

"I haven't heard of anything here."

"The granite for your sidewalks came from this island, but the quarries are only used for swimming now. Carver's the nude quarry."

Frederick sits down on the stone wall of the harbor. Her news doesn't strike him as momentous but the innuendo does. "A nude quarry wasn't on the list of sights I remember," he says almost coyly. He regards his pale body, its sparse hair. Maybe if he doesn't wear his glasses to the quarry, he will be able to forget himself. If he can't see the world, will the world see him?

"I go there sometimes. It's kinda fun."

"I can't imagine people here going in for such things. One thinks of New England as a conservative region."

"Know the sixties?"

He thinks of his street, its monolithic gray apartment houses, Jonah's foldable stroller propped against a struggling, fenced-in tree.

"The nineteen sixties," Dolores smiles. "Nude swimming became popular. We get lots of tourists who still like it, mostly the Europeans, and a few locals. I don't see anything wrong. Nudity is quite natural, you know."

WHERE EVENTS MAY LEAD

He guesses that her mother teaches biology. "One can't disagree with that." He holds up his hands in surrender.

In the long silence, he watches a mother calling to her small tow-headed son, who's climbing on a pile of sinister ex-quarry rocks near the pier. "Come closer," she shouts. "You gone deaf?"

Frederick thinks that he doesn't have an accent of any kind, prep school dulling it, Northwestern smoothing its edges. The islanders' speech sounds so raw and exaggerated to him. He wonders if people can affect group eccentricities.

"We could go there," Dolores offers, her voice taut with promise.

"I'm not sure."

"Well, the other quarry's fine too. Only there are lots of rocks in it and too many people, but I could tell you where it's safe to dive. Why don't I meet you here tomorrow at noon, and we can decide on which one."

"Okay," Frederick says tentatively. He needs film for his camera. Maybe Dolores can take his picture at the pier with its expanse of ocean. Most of his vacation shots are vacant of people. Tonight when he calls Elizabeth at the dude ranch, he'll tell her that he's going swimming and that the locals are friendly.

He stretches out in the lackluster sun, pulls his knees up toward his stomach for balance, and closes his eyes. He can feel Dolores watching him.

"I like your shoes," she's saying.

"They're deck shoes."

"I know. But they're blue. I like 'em."

Frederick brushes Dolores's hand, which she has placed over his eyes like a blindfold.

SIGNS OF DEVOTION

"I'll see you tomorrow," she says, moving backward away from him.

When he sits up to wave good-bye, she's halfway inside the door to Shears.

"It's not so bad that Amy wants to be a nurse," he is assuring Elizabeth on the phone. Elizabeth has this thing about nurses, who are emblems to her of everything wrong in men's treatment of women. "Besides, men are also nurses, and Amy is six. When I was six, I probably wanted to be a fireman."

"More sexist bullshit," Elizabeth shoots back. Not only do vacations make her virulent, but she has recently decided that swearing is all right, and she indulges the habit like the new follower of a creed. "And Jonah calls everything horses. 'It's a bull,' I tell him. 'Mama, horse,' he says."

"Maybe the kid needs glasses."

"I'll have his eyes checked as soon as we get back. Or do you think I should drive him into Jackson Hole?"

Elizabeth treats their children as adults with infirmities. Frederick pictures Jonah wearing a monocle along with his orthopedic Oxfords, which are his punishment for running awkwardly, in Elizabeth's view.

"I'm going swimming tomorrow at a quarry." He won't fill in the details.

"I'm reading a lot."

He pictures her curled in a lounge chair, a book propped on her long, freckled thighs, her tongue wetting her lips in a gesture of concentration.

"Did you know that foot-binding actually damaged the woman so much that she was unable to walk? Slaves or servants had to cart her around. She was a slave of her slaves."

■ 139

"Horrible," Frederick manages, thinking about the quarry. "This is costing a fortune. Give the kids a kiss. I'll call you in two days."

He is afraid to undress because he doesn't want to look at his body before he meets Dolores. He can steam up the room and take a shower in which everything, including himself, will become invisible. But steam can't erase the image of his sprawling self, his heavy legs that can't get tan all at once. He wishes he had a small, compact body, the kind that Frenchmen have, one that can absorb light as evenly as a flat stone. He pulls on his swimming trunks and watches them hang over his thighs. He wonders what one wears to a nude quarry.

Today the children will put on their Western show even though Elizabeth has a drumming headache and is on a crucial chapter of her reading. She has fashioned Amy a cowgirl outfit out of a checkered plastic tablecloth. Jonah will wear his overalls and a cowboy hat she bought him at Jackson Hole. All week Amy has been telling Elizabeth about Hadley: "Hadley knows a neat song. He let us ride our ponies out of the circle. Hadley's a real cowboy."

Elizabeth doubts that real cowboys are counselors for the two-to-six-year-old group. In the New West, many of the cowboys sport designer shirts, chinos, and athletic shoes, as if an ocean and sailboats were tucked behind the austere gray mountains they face at breakfast. She has noticed one authentic-looking cowboy sitting among the college boys in the mess hall. While the Teton Trio played "High Noon" at supper, he appeared to be smiling at her. She felt her lips tug back in acknowledgment. Later she classified it as one of those sympathetic looks that men give to women traveling alone with children. It says, "I'm glad I'm not you." Besides, she doesn't want to make eye contact on her vacation, just read and get away from the kids for six to eight hours a day. She is relieved to be sharing a dining table with a couple from Germany who don't know much English. "*Der Cowboy is auch Singer,*" the tall gangly wife tells her perpetually amused husband. He spends every meal videotaping the cowboys serving them beef tacos, barbecued chicken breasts, and macaroni salad.

It is rumored that a real former astronaut sits at table number one next to Mr. Dennison, the owner, who is fondly referred to as "Big D." Meanwhile, his wife, Little D, runs the kitchen, appearing briefly after the apple brown Betty to beam randomly at the checkered tables.

Elizabeth's headache throbs above her left eye, making her think of Frederick, the locus of her pain. Her summer exiled from him, children in tow like a brave little tugboat, is not her idea. Maybe she should fight for two weeks together, away from the children, instead of traveling two thousand miles in order to pout and read angry feminist tracts. Of course, he'll remind her that they vacation together without the children every January, and that while she doesn't work, he is a pressured attorney who needs time away to relax.

Amy is singing a song about tumbleweed, and a cool breeze is making the cheerful gold corduroy curtains of their cabin puff with air. The place is almost tolerable with its old-fashioned heavy maple furniture, cast-iron washbasins, and sleek hand-held shower and cable TV. It has "authenticity without forsaking comfort." She can't dispute the colorful brochure's claims. Of course, she could stay in New York, but it just doesn't seem fair. Maybe she could send the kids to her mother's in Albany, but they've never been invited. This thought causes a new ray of pain to radiate from her eye. Jonah is pounding his fist on a little drum that the Warriors, his group of two-to-three-year-olds, fashioned out of oatmeal boxes. Elizabeth is braiding Amy's hair, which is too fine, and slips between her fingers. Besides, she is unable to see on the side of her headache. "Forget it, kid. Maybe you can wear a bonnet."

"Hadley says we have to wear—"

"I don't care. Your hair won't go. Tell Hadley that your hair is the last frontier."

"It's not fair! Hadley says!" Amy screams, knocking Jonah over for good measure. He falls on his oatmeal drum, crushing it, and begins to sob, his little shoulders hunching in and out for emphasis.

"Hadley—"

"I don't care. Tell him to leave us alone," Elizabeth is saying when a voice interrupts with, "Anybody home?"

"Hi!" Amy shouts to Hadley Incarnate. Running to the door, she hugs his waist. "Mom, this is Hadley."

If she stands up too fast, she might vomit. "Pleased to meet you," she says, twisting her neck forty-five degrees toward him.

She's noticed Hadley at dinner. He has an open face, handsome without being showy. He is delicate, and all his features seem miniature; small green eyes, a careful nose, thin lips. Nothing has grown to the point that Hadley will have to excuse himself for possessing it. It is a face one can admire without being effusive. She wouldn't even have noticed it in the Guggenheim or Bloomingdale's. But on vacation, encouraged by the novels she'd read as a stalky, unpopular teenager, in which girls have summer romances with stevedores, carnies, and cowboys, and by Frederick's ostentatious absence, Hadley's face can lead her anywhere.

She forces herself to rise for introductions, preserving a distance from him so that perspective can work in her favor. Clearly, she may be taller than him by half a foot, but across the room, it is hard to judge. Assuming her best maternal pose, she slouches over Jonah, who is still moaning, and beams at Amy. "I'm Elizabeth."

"Aren't you feeling well?"

"I have a terrible headache. I think it's allergies."

"That's odd. I come here summers because my allergies improve so much. I live in Los Angeles. The pollen count goes off the scale there."

So they have a bond of rashes, running noses, drumming sinuses, and watery eyes. "We're from New York." Elizabeth manages a smile that divides her face into the well and the unwell.

"I can tell by your accent," he laughs. "Can I get you anything? I have some allergy pills. They're prescription, but I don't suppose they'd hurt."

"Would you mind?"

"No problem. I'll take Amy along. She's always wanted to see where the cowboys live."

Has he used the word *cowboys* ironically? Is he propositioning her six year-old daughter? She guesses not. She guesses that none of his words have any meaning beyond their registered intent.

• • •

WHERE EVENTS MAY LEAD

The evening sun has a way of setting on the island that reminds Frederick of cardboard scenery. One minute it will flood the bay with colors; the next minute it is gone, as if a prop man went home early with the essential scenery. He has noticed this summer how things bump along, having little flow. Even the moon, which he's observed nightly while still in New York, adds its portion in childish increments. He hardly ever considers landscape, but tonight it concerns him. Lying naked in his motel room at the Tides, he imagines how he might have looked if he had been bold enough to go with Dolores to Carver's. Instead, he'd offered to buy her a crab roll at Roonie's. They'd sat in a booth where initials had been carved over initials, a palimpsest of mundane meals.

"My dad might be going to Carver's today anyway. Wednesday's his day off."

"Does your mom know your dad goes there?"

Dolores laughed pleasantly. "It's hard to hide a full body tan."

She'd smiled at him a lot and promised to meet him for lunch Thursday, but lying in the motel room, listening to the waves catch under the bridge at the Mill Race Inn next door, Frederick knows he won't see her again. He takes a huge blue sleeping pill, and before falling into his black dreamless hole, resolves to leave the island tomorrow. It is too confining here. The geography conspires to make him feel inadequate. The only large impersonal place is the ocean, which is too cold for swimming, and over-fished; and Dolores is sixteen. Tomorrow he'll call Elizabeth and take a flight out from Portland. She'll probably welcome his company. Maybe these summers apart are a little self-indulgent.

SIGNS OF DEVOTION

Will he remember his resolution in the morning? he wonders, as he covers his head and lets out several soothing, sleep-inducing sighs.

The children's program is an unqualified success. Even people without children are here to see the Wild West in Song and Skit. Amy, without braids, is Annie Oakley. Hadley settled on pigtails out of sympathy for Elizabeth, not because he'd lowered his standards. He is a demanding director. Do people realize the difficulty of getting children to speak loudly and clearly? Hadley has succeeded. Elizabeth sees his uncomplicated eyes shining toward hers as even Jonah, whose part is to sing the last Indian in "Ten Little Indians," makes a gallant effort to pronounce his r's. "No maw Indian boyers," he shouts at the German's video camera, and Hadley beams.

The two allergy pills haven't worked on her headache, but they have made Elizabeth too punchy to care. She can concentrate on events only through great effort, which, she notices, is a way of fine-tuning the essentials. With unexpected power, she orders Amy and Jonah to take a nap before the chuck wagon cookout.

She leaves the cabin to find Hadley. The bunkhouse where he stays is actually a series of small bedrooms with washrooms and a shared, gloomy lounge. His bunk is number 7, he had told her after the program. The rooms smell of paint, and she sees two buckets outside of room number 4. The color is champagne semi-gloss. She imagines a college boy spending his off-hours painting the walls of his temporary quarters a more appealing color. She wonders why people take such enormous efforts with their surroundings when there is so little energy in one's supply.

"Hi!" Hadley smiles.

"I thought I'd see where the real cowboys live," Elizabeth says tentatively.

Hadley laughs. "Your kids were super, especially Amy. She can really sing." He takes a Coors out of a cooler near the door and hands it to Elizabeth. "Come in."

"Thanks," she says, taking the opened can. "You work so well with children. You must love them."

"Well, it's part of my philosophy."

The word makes Elizabeth flinch. There's nothing worse than a college junior with a philosophy. When Elizabeth doesn't ask what his philosophy might be after the expected interval, Hadley continues.

"I think that if you show people you think the most of them, they'll give the most to you."

Instead of agreeing, Elizabeth asks if he's a business major.

"Management engineering. I hope to work for a big firm, but human service also interests me. You can't take the human element out of business." He glows at her, a Buddha of the Private Sector.

"So this is where the cowboys live," Elizabeth repeats almost to herself and laughs.

"Yeah," Hadley says, smiling quizzically. Then he lunges at her mouth, kissing her precisely. Hadley's small hands massage her back and slip down her behind, which he cups in his hands.

"I have a bed," he says.

"I suppose you do." He moves to kiss her again, and before she can decide what her next act will be, he's helping her remove her shirt and bra in several efficient strokes. She throws her skirt and underpants onto his speckled linoleum floor.

"Hadley, I can't find my mom," Amy is saying. She has Jonah in tow, still barefoot and sucking sleepily on his two middle fingers.

Hadley points to his wall, which Elizabeth faces, asleep. His cowboy-motif bedspread covers her shoulders. Hadley hopes that he's blocking Amy's view of her mother's clothing. Holding his finger to his mouth, he whispers, "The allergy pill made your mom drowsy. I told her to take a little nap."

Though the story might end here, readers often worry about the aftermath. It's especially perilous to leave two adults asleep, estranged by temperament, habit, and geography, so here is the epilogue: If Frederick holds to his resolve to join his family a continent away, Amy will tell him that he shouldn't have missed her starring role as Annie Oakley. While Elizabeth pales, Frederick, never good at discerning her moods, hugs Amy and plays with her fine mousy hair. He feels his heart strain with regret and vows to repay his children with his animated presence in the future. Amy adds that Hadley ("their counselor," Elizabeth breathlessly explains) treated her to a banana split. "Me too," Jonah states with such animation that he tumbles off a step and bumps his head. In the comforting of the child and the getting of the ice that ensues, Amy loses the thread of her story. She will not recount that the ice cream outing occurred while her mother slept naked under Hadley's bedspread.

But, since memory has an odd way of reinsinuating itself like a vengeful distant relative, Amy may recall those details later, causing Elizabeth to anticipate a vigorously entertaining digression. In fact, the whole incident improves Elizabeth's imaginative capacity. Waiting constantly to be exposed by some trivial circumstance of Amy's recollection, she perfects anecdotes for every social occasion and a melting way of looking at Frederick that says, "You'll never want to go away without me again."

Around Christmas, she is is observed telling stories at Frederick's business gatherings and regaling the party-goers, even those in the remotest corner. People remark to Frederick that they never knew Elizabeth to be so entertaining, and Frederick thinks that his wife has grown into a mature and charming woman. Remembering Dolores now and then, he'll decide that a sixteen-year-old with a vulnerably thin neck can't match up to this formidable, confident wife with long freckled thighs under her tasteful crepe suit, this source of growing pride and desire.

If, however, Frederick's untormented sleep weakens his resolve to join Elizabeth at the Big D Family Resort just outside of Jackson Hole, I can't be held responsible for where events may lead.

KABUKI EVERYTHING

"The clumsier you are, the more you need the passive voice," Nora told the doctor setting her wrist. Since he didn't respond, she reclassified him from sympathetic to possibly demented. It was midnight in the emergency room. Two fluorescent tubes pulsed above her head to the crying of the woman in the next cubicle. Nora overheard that the woman's daughter had torn off the back door while high on cocaine. Nora wondered if the woman behind the partition was accompanied by her daughter or the door on its bent hinges. She wondered about her own strength. Could she tear off a door? Even as a sixteen-year-old, had she ever been that angry? There had been one scene with her father involving curses at 1 A.M. Neighbors had heard them through open windows on an early-June evening. She recalled the time of year because the issue had been whether she could ride Jordan Howser's motorbike. She wouldn't depict the scene as an angry one, more a surprising breach in the distance that characterized her relationship with her father. They had no more right shouting at each other than strangers on a subway. Quietly embarrassed, her father had called her from work the next day to apologize.

Nora asked the doctor if many violent people were brought through the doors. The doctor didn't respond. Nora began to wonder if he understood English. Rather than test him, she thought about emergency-room telephones, where many desperate calls are made. She thought of calling Katy, or Warren, away in Boston, to tell them of her injury. She thought of calling her mother, who'd be asleep in New York. She thought of calling several old school chums, who'd laugh at her clumsiness, foreshadowed in her youth. One of the problems with Warren's being out of town was that a trip to the emergency room was supposed to be a family outing. Even the patient next to her had a daughter to bemoan. All Nora had was an agenda for tomorrow, which would include telling her story.

When she got home, there were three messages on her answering machine. The first was from Katy, who'd apparently been insulted.

"Since it is a free country, can't the Weeping Virgin be viewed without sarcasm by a friend whose taste, more often than not, is questionable?"

Katy was right. Without resentment, with a look of nothing more than bemusement, Katy had accompanied Nora to a comedy club where a woman professing to be Woody Allen's first wife, the one who hadn't gotten into movies, was performing. Nora had wanted desperately to go, imagining it would be like seeing T. S. Eliot's wife give a poetry reading.

Her entire act consisted of Woody Allen jokes, followed by Louise Lasser jokes, followed by Diane Keaton and Mia Farrow jokes. At first it seemed funny in a fragile way, but then Nora got nervous for her. She began to feel like a helicopter pilot trying to land on a hatchery. She remembered a terrible time in Sunday school when she had told the rabbi she didn't believe in God and he'd pretended not to hear.

SIGNS OF DEVOTION

Another time in college she'd gotten drunk and passed out in an Italian neighborhood. When she woke up, she was encircled by nine-year-olds, who must have thought they'd found a mermaid on their sidewalk. Both experiences had left her feeling powerful and stupid. She wondered if she'd felt worse than Woody Allen's first wife, who, as the act wore on, became less and less convincing.

"She was a fake," Katy offered with no malice in her voice. She stated it as a fact.

"Maybe she knew Woody Allen."

"Or saw one of his movies."

"He deserves to be slandered in jokes."

The second message was from Rowan, her boss at the children's textbook firm.

"You can't put an Eskimo in a kayak, Nora. You know very well that it would suggest a racial stereotype and never pass committee. I suggest we put a black woman in the kayak. Think about it."

Nora imagined a generation of fifth graders thinking Eskimos are black. She pictured Martin Luther King, Jr., portrayed as an Eskimo. The job annoyed her constantly. She couldn't discuss dinosaurs, which creationists view as a figment of the liberal imagination. She couldn't make mythological or biblical allusions either. Once she had tried a disguised reference to Adam and Eve devoured by monsters on their first day out of the Garden. "Keep it up," Rowan had said, "and you'll be back to your dogs."

Rowan referred to Nora's previous career as a grief therapist for pet loss. She had lived in California then, and the job offered short hours and good pay. The only trouble with the job was grief. People took it harder when their pets died than she'd expected. Marriages broke up over it, especially childless ones. Kids got neglected for years, and the guilt of the surviving pet sometimes became unbearable. There were actual cases of remaining pets committing suicide. Nora's job was explaining the danger signs. One Labrador began gnawing on poisonous plants. She advised the couple to weed their garden and keep him on a tight leash. "For the sake of Lips," Nora implored, "give up your grief."

"Lips!" the husband replied passionately, but Nora could tell by the reticent way that he handled the dog that the three were bent on disaster. She finally grew to hate the business.

After moving to Chicago, she met Rowan in a bar called Dr. No. He offered to sleep with her, which she refused. She offered him her mind in business. Since then, she'd been writing children's textbooks devoid of racial, ethnic, religious, or sexual controversy. All she could tell were stories about runaway mutts, but she left out the suicidal owners and self-abusive pets.

The third message was from Warren. She could tell because their machine annoyed him into sighing. He'd pause, sigh, and get his revenge by recording possibly the worst pun known to man.

"Who made the mess in Mesopotamia?"

Nora could have turned off the machine before it had the chance, but even his voice gave her pleasure. Despite the late hour, she'd return the calls, first to Katy out of duty and then to Warren as reward.

"Sure, it's a free country," Nora told Katy. "You're free to waste any Sunday you want on a religious miracle. I'm free to think that the last miracle in America happened when

Richard Nixon was forced to leave office, but I'd have to qualify that as a mere secular wonder. He got to ride away, waving like a good boy on his birthday."

"Where were you tonight? I thought of calling Warren."

"I was having my wrist set. I was trying to reach a teapot and fell off a stepstool onto the dishwasher. I know that mankind in general is getting taller, but the Greens haven't ascended a single inch. My genes are frankly retrograde."

"This is all very funny," Katy said in her Anglicized Polish accent. She had lived in America only six years.

"I think it's funny too. I told the doctor how funny it was, and he stared at me like a cold egg on a plate. Don't you hate that patronizing look they give you?"

"Maybe to doctors, emergency rooms are entertaining in and of themselves. They need no patients to make them feel comfortable."

"I forgot," Nora said. She was referring to Katy's Polish training as a surgeon.

"Jess will come along tomorrow," Katy says.

"To see the Weeping Virgin?"

"Yes, he says that he's interested."

"Great!" Nora says.

Jess was a real psychopath, and Katy was his wife. Sometimes Nora was scared not just for Katy but for knowing Katy. Someday Katy would do something Jess perceived as insulting and a Minicam would be sent. Maybe a SWAT team. Once he'd torn up a dress that he thought Katy had worn too often. Once he'd turned off a Cubs game during an aerial view of Wrigley Field because he hated the cameraman's pretensions to art. Katy offered no resistance. Just as she thought that Nora was colorful because she was

KABUKI EVERYTHING

American, she thought that Jess was temperamental because he was an artist.

Nora called Warren. "I'm not up on the Old Testament," she began.

"Meaning?"

"I don't know who made the mess. I could guess it was probably God, who's always angry at some king for being filled with pride. As soon as you feel it, you melt gold into idol molds, and all hell breaks loose."

"You're really popping tonight."

Nora could picture Warren's long, intelligent face, his look of amused impatience. "It's because of my brush with death. I broke my wrist. The intern who set it appeared to be deaf. What's more, I'm going to be healed tomorrow in a church on South Kildare, where a pipe is leaking and people are calling it a miracle."

"Another Katy special?"

"And Jess is going too. The gang of three. Want to fly in and join us?"

"I'd rather die in my sleep."

"You shouldn't say such things. It tempts fate. Don't you remember dares in high school?"

"Do you think a cosmic force is listening to our phone conversation?"

"Better not depersonalize it. Give it a pronoun."

"Would it mind if I come home tomorrow night?"

"I'm glad it's just my wrist this time." Two winters ago Nora had broken her kneecap. Warren required the humility of three saints to live through that injury.

• • •

Before he accompanied his wife on her latest folly, this time a religious one, Jess would visit Mimi, the student he saw every Sunday morning while Katy, assuming that he was working at his studio, slept late or went to church. Jess believed that, to most artists, studios are an excuse for philandering. Weren't even the Great Masters sexually active?

At Mimi's he turned into subject, having his nude portrait painted on her lead-gray futon. Mimi was a lover of angles and more intense about her work than Jess had been in years. No matter that she portrayed sawhorses for legs, praying-mantis arms, an ax for a face. The portrait wouldn't be very good. Given twenty years of Sundays, many lovers, Mimi might be able to correct her vision as a golfer does his stroke. Jess thought it was too late for him to do the same. A string of young art students would have to work harder to provide him with a svelte form as years passed. He'd better prepare himself for old age by getting serious. In the event that Sundays meant a return to his studio, he'd need something to do there.

"Maybe I'll try sculpture," he said to Mimi.

"I thought you're a painter," she said listlessly.

To change the subject, Jess began imagining an evening out with this young woman so intent on herself that she hardly noticed him. Why did he have so much enthusiasm for lying to Katy on Mimi's behalf? He'd already arranged an alibi, an art opening; a place, the Demme Street Gallery; and a scenario for Katy to decline. It was his colleague Loren's opening. Katy had no sympathy for Loren, who was her idea of a spoiled American. It would make her repressed Marxism literally burst forth just to hear him mentioned.

KABUKI EVERYTHING

"So the spoiled little brat has finished three paintings? Did his mother help him? Did the government take food from hungry children's mouths to give him a grant?" She wouldn't want any part of the evening, the actual details of which Jess pictured as an avant-garde soap opera. First, dinner at a post-industrial restaurant, where he'd demonstrate his expertise in domestic-wine selection. They'd take in a play, maybe the Kabuki *Moby Dick* being done at a local theater with a national reputation. Then back to Mimi's, where they'd make love like new, culturally advanced people.

"Imagine all the whiteface they'll need for the whale," Jess offered after introducing the subject of the play.

"The whale's already white," Mimi said without looking up.

One thing that was clear, he needn't be funny on her behalf.

"Want some coffee?" Mimi said. She'd walked over to Jess and kissed him on the cheek.

"Sisterly at best."

Mimi took a small white hand and rubbed blue paint across his cheek.

"I like your hands."

"So do I. Have you ever noticed that Hockney can't paint hands?"

Jess felt a longing pulling like a rope at his groin. "We could take a break," he said.

"I have a schedule to keep." She winked. Then she went back to the canvas. Her diligence at small tasks reminded him of Katy putting on makeup or cutting bread. She'd look almost cross-eyed with effort, her tongue serving as metronome and pointer.

SIGNS OF DEVOTION

Sometimes at Mimi's he loved Katy more than he understood. He also felt disappointed for her. To escape a Communist country where even sugar is rationed to wind up with a jerk like him. Not only had they been unable to have a child during four years of marriage, but she had also failed to get certified to practice medicine. In Poland she could wear surgical gloves and change the rhythm of a man's heart. Here she could only swear in Polish and cry bitterly when Jess or her job at the medical lab got to be too much for her.

Mimi hooked her leg over Jess's and slid behind him on the futon. He must have fallen asleep because he hadn't seen her take her clothes off. He saw blue dots of paint near his nipples and on his forearm. He wondered what she had been doing while she slept.

Nora would have called the drive to the church almost congenial, given that Jess was driving, that it was raining, and that Katy was staring into her lap.

"I've read a few reports on the statue. The disbelievers think it's a leaky pipe that's causing the moisture," Nora says.

"That's one possibility," Katy said. "The other is a miracle."

"Katy believes in miracles, Nora. She's a peasant, remember, with a deeply superstitious nature. While we were in American schools learning how many yards are in a football field, Katy was being told that women can give you the evil eye and cause your children to have tails."

"That is nonsense, Jess. I too was learning science. I am no less scientific than you. You think that money is magic.

KABUKI EVERYTHING

You think that food appears on our table by magic. Who here is the peasant?"

"Haven't you heard of the *Scientific American?* That's me."

Nora and Katy laughed.

"Nora, have you seen the Kabuki *Moby Dick?* I bet they need a lot of whiteface for the whale."

"That theater should change its name to Kabuki Everything." Nora realized that all three of them were laughing. She wished there were some way to record the moment for posterity.

The line to see the Weeping Virgin stretched around the corner of Kildare onto Harlem. Listless policemen patrolled the area.

"Imagine a street named after Richard Chamberlain," Nora told Katy.

"Shogun Street?"

"Didn't they have the 'Doctor Kildare' show in Warsaw?"

"No, we saw "The Dr. Wozniak Hour," a helpful reminder to use our coupons for healthy food, to dress warmly in winter, and to keep down our vodka consumption."

Then she laughed, which obviously annoyed Jess, who'd been waiting in line too long as soon as they arrived. Nora couldn't figure out why he'd joined them. Maybe his work at the studio wasn't going well. Maybe he was having an affair and felt guilty enough to try to please Katy. Nora tried to discern a telltale sign of pleasure on his face, but Jess's features wouldn't be transformed by love. There was a hardness around his eyes that might be called attractive. In some men it would be a mark of intensity. In Jess it was merely intransigence turning his face to stone.

SIGNS OF DEVOTION

Nora began surveying the crowd. She thought of herself as a tourist among the devout. Even the dull-eyed policemen appeared to be more guileless. She smiled to think that maybe her interpretation was wrong. Couldn't everyone in line be a painter like Jess, looking for a naive subject, or a writer like herself, researching a feature story called "Religious Ecstasy in Working-Class America"? She saw no sign of ecstasy in the crowd, comprised mostly of elderly women in polyester suits and rain bonnets. Sometimes there appeared to be pockets of joy but mainly among the children, happy to be out in the rain. Most everyone appeared weary. Even if the Virgin cried real tears, it was probably too late for many of them. At other times in a crowd, Nora had felt a comforting unanimity of spirit. Here she sensed only resignation to the slow snaking line in the December mist.

She looked for people she knew, fixing her eyes on a group of women about her age. She could tell by their well-scrubbed skin, their close- cropped hair, the uniform drabness of their street clothes, and their comportment that they were nuns. She thought of Sister Cecile, her brother's former girlfriend Terry Onofrio, who had become a nun/performance artist after leaving Ronny. Couldn't she have joined the Peace Corps to make a statement? Did she have to take a vow and marry Jesus to escape Nora's chronically depressed brother, who sold hearing aids? Nora could still see Ronny in a summer haircut at Coney Island, tanner and more promising than his friends. What happened as people got older? Could a single synapse misfire and capsize a life? If Nora ever got to the statue, she'd ask it to help Ronny and Terry individually.

The man in front of them was crying. He was sobbing

outwardly, and the strong December wind that picked up speed when they'd turned the corner blew the tears off his face sideways toward the curb. He appeared to be alone. As more people noticed him, it became a pressing and embarrassing fact. Part of the afternoon's message was stoicism. How many people were in line with a crushing problem to discuss? That the statue itself was reported to be crying made it a greater obligation for the crowd to keep a stiff upper lip.

"It's your fault," the man was saying to Katy.

"Pardon me," Katy said, in the sincerely interested manner that told Nora she'd have made a good doctor.

"It's your fault," the man repeated. This time his voice was raised and people in line were beginning to move away from them.

"Stop bothering her," Nora demanded. She looked at Katy, whose eyes were wide with incomprehension and whose color had become high and blotchy.

"It's her fault," the man told Jess. "She fucks things up for me."

"Katy, do you know this guy?"

"Not in my life," she said, American idioms deserting her.

"It's hard to believe you don't know him."

Leave it to Jess to side with the lunatic. Nora took Jess aside. "Don't you know how many nuts per square inch are in line to see this statue?"

Jess hesitated a minute, then repeated, "Do you know my wife?"

"She's ruined everything," the man repeated. Then he broke down and wept long enough for Nora to grasp Katy's shoulder and lead her toward the car.

"C'mon, Katy. Let's get out of the cold."

As soon as Katy unlocked the car, she buried her face in the steering wheel. Her crying continued as Nora looked out the window for Jess. She still could observe him in line. He appeared to be comforting the man. Both bent their heads solemnly. The way their arms were similarly crossed and their bodies leaned toward each other suggested commiseration.

Katy finally spoke. "Only in America can I find a husband who is so democratic that he believes a madman."

Nora couldn't imagine what she should say. She tried a grief therapy mini-speech about getting over losses.

"*Piou-piou,*" Katy replied.

"What did you say?"

"What a French poodle would say to your speech."

Nora caught Katy's eye, and they broke into the kind of tense laughter one might hear in an emergency room. Then they stopped looking at each other.

Nora couldn't see Jess's face or the stranger's as they made their way to the chapel door, but she was sure that Jess was telling him that women always fuck things up. If you wait long enough, it happens.

CALIFORNIA

■ ■ ■ ■ ■ ■ ■ ■ ■ Cal Weathers liked Oleg Lum because of his name. Nothing else recommended the earnest Russian who shucked oysters next to Cal at The Shell. Since Oleg's arrival, no one joked about Cal's name being California or asked him about the weather on the coast. Instead, they said, "Oh, Leg!" when the worst kitchen jobs had to be performed. Just seeing Oleg display his incompetence boldly as a badge made Cal smile.

"What is funny?" Oleg would ask.

"You, man," Cal would answer, shaking his head and letting another gritty oyster slither onto the shaved ice.

When they had finished their early-morning shifts as salad preparers, Cal and Oleg would wash their hands with Boraxo and take their lunches to the card table covered with red oilcloth where the help ate, that is, if Mr. Perke wasn't around. Sometimes the table would be cluttered with week-old guest checks that Mr. Perke totaled on an ancient adding machine, which trailed a pink column of numbers onto the floor.

"They're giving the place away!" he'd wail mostly to himself and then add, "Damn bitches!" to include any employee who had the potential to tote up a check incorrectly.

"Is good food," Oleg commented over his plate of perch and grayish peas.

"Is beginning to stink," Cal mimicked.

CALIFORNIA

At first Oleg hadn't been sure he liked Cal. Cal looked menacing to Oleg, who'd seen so few black people before he left Russia. He remembered Tesfaye, an Ethiopian student he'd known in Moscow. How fascinated he'd been to observe the cold Russian air circulating through Tesfaye's lungs and out of his thin, fine nose. There was nothing about Cal that Oleg would call refined. His jaw had been broken and was jerry-rigged to the rest of his face. Oleg wondered what held it there. Cal's hands also frightened him, seeming too large to connect at his thin wrists. The wrists led to bulging forearms. His arms seemed wasted at the restaurant. Oleg imagined them better serving an iron worker.

Sometimes their lunch hours were taken up by Cal's political tirades. He always talked low so that Mr. Perke could only imagine what he was telling Oleg. Oleg would lean across the table to catch Cal's words.

"See President Peckerwood last night on TV?"

"You mean U.S. President?"

"President Peckerwood. Lives in the Bird House."

"I saw news of President's trip to Rome."

"Peckerwood's always smiling like he's smelling sweet shit. His wife's real hot. He divorced his first wife because she got fat. Republicans don't like that."

"Is true?"

"I read all about it. Don't you read books, Oleg? How do you imagine you're going to make your way in Peckerland?"

Oleg reached for more tartar sauce and stared at his plate. He was afraid when Cal spoke this way.

"Is wonderful country where you can call President bad language."

"Ain't it great? We elect rat brains like him so we can exercise our right to complain. Have you read up on it? I was just going to use mine to tell Perke that I want Saturday off. My grandma died again."

"I am sorry to hear. She was ill?"

"She was dead. Been dead since last time I wanted Saturday off. If Perke had a memory, waitresses wouldn't steal him blind. You watch. I'll ask, and he'll say fine."

Each day when Oleg left work he called Claire, the beautiful American he'd met in the summer. If he were seeing Claire in Moscow, he'd know it was serious. But here in America he didn't know what it meant that a divorced woman and her ten-year-old daughter had taken a liking to him. By the way they cooed and smirked in his presence, it might mean that he was entertaining, like a talking parrot with an accent.

"Today it's weaving," Carrie explained to Oleg. "My mom's on a real self-improvement kick. She's taking a class in making Christmas cookies, and we're Jewish! I'll tell her you called again, Oleg."

"She is unhappy that I call?"

"No, wants you to come to dinner again, Oleg. She thinks you're interesting."

"Let's get ripped," Cal said to Oleg after they finished Thursday's shift.

"I do not understand."

"What do you Russkies understand? Do you understand vodka?"

"Is great painkiller," Oleg said quietly. He was afraid that

CALIFORNIA

Mr. Perke planted spies among the kitchen help and that he was in imminent danger of losing his job for talking about sordid topics.

"Get ripped. Drink vodka." Cal raised an imaginary shot glass to his lips. When he thought Oleg didn't understand, he became monosyllabic.

"Drinking is sometimes good," Oleg continued, "but today I am busy. I must talk to Claire, who looks like beautiful Indian princess. She is my friend."

"Good for you."

"And I am worried about story I read in paper." Oleg pulled a folded scrap of newsprint from his pocket and buried his eyes in it. "Baby is left on train downtown. He is not owned by parents but in foster home. What is foster home, Cal?"

"It's like a parking lot for kids."

"I would own this baby, or Claire, who can have no more babies."

"What are you talking about, man? C'mon, Oleg. We can have drinks and then we'll talk about babies. My old lady moved out on me with my three babies. Lamont's the oldest. He looks like me before I got my new chin. Fred's in the middle. He's mean like his momma. Baby Cal's just like me. He's only three. It's not true you love yours all the same."

"You must be proud father, Cal. I was married to getting out of Russia, idea that owned me like wife. I work very hard, and now I am here."

"C'mon, I'll buy you a few drinks next door. We'll watch a little TV."

"Is okay, Cal. I drink with you, and then maybe we find baby even today."

SIGNS OF DEVOTION

"It can happen that fast, Oleg. A baby can be lost or found in no time. Once this dude I know named Harold was staying at his old lady's. She had to go to work, so Harold says he'll watch the kid. Baby's no older than two. So Harold's been up all night. He's watching the baby. Then he hears, 'Wake up! You're under arrest!' Seems he fell asleep and the baby walked right out the front door. Two cops found him standing in front of Comiskey Park."

"It happened for this baby on el train last night where maybe drug-taking parents leave him. 'Get lost baby from train,' I will tell Claire. Or maybe I get baby and give to her as gift."

After toasting the recent improvement of American and Russian relations, President Peckerwood and his wife, Claire, Carrie, Lamont and Baby Cal, they started on toasts for improvement. Oleg wished that Cal's middle son would prove acceptable. Cal wished that Oleg would procure his baby.

"People think that guys wanting babies are a little funny, Oleg. You know, there was a guy who dressed like a clown and killed boys."

Oleg looked indignant. "Is not my hope to be killing clown."

"People think the worst. For instance, the first day I saw you, I thought you'd be a real loser. People is prejudiced."

"I go to police and explain. I say baby is like bicycle. If found and no owner, I can buy."

"I'd just say you'd like to know the whereabouts of the baby on the news."

"Okay, we say that."

"We?"

"Cal and Oleg say that to officers."

"What good will I do? 'Who's he?' they'll ask. 'Your good thang?' No, you go alone and act real serious, like you're in a white people's church."

"Okay, I say, 'Police, do not give baby to bad parents, who leave it behind, or to false parents."

"I'd be cool, Oleg. If you say things like *false*, they'll get all riled up, and you won't get a thing."

"Maybe I should wait for Claire?"

"Sure, we'll have more drinks. Then Claire can go with you. Police can't resist mothers. Once when I was incarcerated, my mother came. Ten minutes later I was walking."

"You are then criminal?"

"Everyone's a criminal, Oleg. You just need a little time and less money, and you'll be one too."

Oleg had seen the ring in a pawnshop on Devon Avenue. Pawnshops were sadder to him than anything else about America. No one could convince Oleg that possessions weren't loved. He remembered the transistor radio he'd bought on the black market in Moscow. It was shaped like a Coke bottle. For many years it had been his skyline. It wasn't the object itself but the owner's feelings for it. The sillier the object, the better. The more ostentatious, the better. The more one needed to sacrifice for it, the better. The more degraded its surroundings, the better it looked in contrast.

The ring was the perfect embodiment of useless pleasure. The thought of wearing it while shucking oysters in the smoky restaurant delighted him. He'd waited a month for the owner to repossess it, but it was still in the window on the day he'd set for the purchase.

SIGNS OF DEVOTION

He hoped the ring would purge his current mood, the darkest he'd felt since he'd left Russia. The desolation of September with the beaches closing, Carrie back in school, Claire busy with her life, and his new job at The Shell left him wondering if he'd left Russia at all, or if Russia was a malady one had for a lifetime, a chill from the tundra producing visions of imminent doom. Even the letters he wrote to the newspaper's "Personal View" column were colored by his new bitterness, a word he thought he'd left behind. Sometimes Carrie's ten-year-old nonchalance annoyed him. The world had no time for ambivalence, he wanted to tell her. Lots of people needed to be warned to change their lives.

Nothing was worse than official thugs, not even the thugs that remove cars from parking lots after disconnecting the finely tuned alarm systems. Thieves were in business for themselves. They were committed personally to Free Enterprise. They risked their lives for shiny fenders, leather seats, and metallic-blue paint. The police risked their lives for a paycheck. They interfered with the individual's religious urge toward ownership. It was hard to understand how a free country could tolerate such purveyors of injustice.

When Oleg first shopped in American markets, he wondered why his fellow émigrés always bought the brashest colors of toilet paper. Then he remembered the toilet-paper queues in Russia. If there were orange toilet paper in America or red with sequins, all the better. It was beautiful to waste beauty. He began winking at old women, so spare in the rest of their shopping. Their carts contained generic cans, cream cheese, and the beautiful toilet paper, usually

CALIFORNIA

in shocking pink. Oleg made a mental note to write a new "Personal View" column. Toilet paper might well be the subject.

Upon entering the pawnshop, he took an immediate dislike to the clerk. He was perhaps twenty-five and had thinning hair. His face looked refined, and his eyes were small and alert when he glanced up from his newspaper. Why didn't Americans, charged with the most awesome responsibilities, show any enthusiasm for their jobs? He'd give anything to buy back loved items from desperate people and sell them to ardent new owners. People didn't understand the drama or pathos of their own lives. Once he'd seen a man sitting on a gray couch on the sidewalk amid his belongings. When a neighbor explained to Oleg that the man had been evicted, Oleg was amazed by the man's calm reserve. Why didn't people beat their breasts in indignation?

"May I help you?" the young man was repeating.

"I am interested, please, in the diamond for the hand."

"The Mason's ring? It's a good one, a real one." The young man theatrically displayed a jewel-inspecting device that reminded Oleg of a periscope.

"Please, I can use?" Oleg put the instrument to his eye and enjoyed the prismatic effect of the stone.

"I'll give it to you for four fifty. You can pay it all at once or put down a hundred."

"Please, I can try it on?"

"Sorry, sir. I can let you try on another ring in the same size, but our diamond jewelry isn't available for wearing before purchase. It's part of our new loss-prevention plan."

Maybe all the cameras in the window were burglary devices, and the mindless television screens contained video-

SIGNS OF DEVOTION

recording equipment. Maybe the man behind the barred window had a gun trained on him. Oleg's left temple throbbed.

The man handed Oleg a discolored silver circle the same size as the ring. It fit him snugly. "Now I am married to loss prevention."

"You can put a hundred dollars down and sign a contract to pay the rest on time. We offer twenty-one percent financing, which is very good these days, and we have a thirty-day return policy. If you decide to return the ring within that period of time, you can have your money back minus a twenty-dollar handling fee. Here are the papers explaining this method of payment."

"And if the ring is wanted by old owner?"

"Once the ring is sold, it's yours. Previous ownership is invalidated. You know, *no backsies*, as we used to say in marbles."

"Is this U.S. law?"

"I don't imagine that I represent the views of the whole government. Pawnshop law is different."

"I will pay hundred dollars and sign mortgage document."

Oleg signed the papers in triplicate, bought an old Brownie camera for Carrie and a digital alarm for Claire. As he carried the items out of the store, he couldn't take his eyes off his hand.

In the few hours that remained before dinner, he'd work on a "Personal View" article for the paper.

Dear Personal View:

Pawnshop law is very good American practice according to Oleg Lum, who purchased diamond from tragic Mason who cannot keep what he loves. I think too that pawnshop law *would be valuable justice tool in missing child cases. Parents get certain time to claim lost child. If child is unclaimed, then any person who has $450, the price of beautiful Mason ring, can own child. There is no need for police in Pawnshop Adoption Plan. It can be business deal involving no backsies. One could sign contract from listless pawnshop man and baby would benefit from new owner who loves his possession.*

Thank you,
Oleg Lum

At nine o'clock they decided to begin dinner, even though Cal hadn't arrived.

"Cal is casual man," Oleg assured Carrie and Claire, who were more hungry than interested in the personality of Oleg's new friend. "He is sometimes late for work and sometimes leaves early. He is sometimes sober and sometimes not. Maybe today is not sober day, or one of his three handsome sons has trouble and Cal must play parole officer."

"Are his kids in prison?" Carrie asked.

"No, is little joke I make about school for you, Carrie."

"Oleg, I bought some tickets for a flute concert. Would you like to join us on Sunday?"

"I am delighted to go to concert and to wear my new ring from beautiful land of dreams, pawnshop."

"You got our things at a pawnshop? Aren't things at pawnshops stolen?"

"Is not stolen but sacrificed. The new owners buy and love more than old ones. Like baby I see on news. He is left on el train. He needs new owner, Claire."

"I saw that story too, Oleg. Imagine leaving a baby alone on a train riding back and forth all night. It's so sad."

SIGNS OF DEVOTION

"Maybe you or I could help him?"

"How could we, Oleg?"

"We could say that he is our baby."

"But he isn't our baby. Why would we say that about a lost baby?"

"We could find him."

"Adopt him?"

"Yes."

Carrie dug her fork into her mashed potatoes. "You want my mom to keep this baby, Oleg?"

"Is lost baby. Is lost without us."

"They'll find him a good home, Oleg. You shouldn't worry about so many things." Claire grasped his knuckle and looked puzzled, then amused. "Maybe you need a pet," she said quietly.

"A dog or cat?" Carrie asked.

"Cal says police can get child. That we go to police together. Once when Cal needed release, his mother came and won his freedom."

"This guy's a criminal?" Carrie shrieked joyously. "What did he do?"

"Little Carrie, everyone in America is criminal if he has less money and little time. I have much money to spend on regaining baby."

"You'd need a lawyer, not the police, Oleg. And there's little chance that a bachelor so new to this country would qualify to adopt a child."

"There are many babies needing homes. I am good shopper. I want the baby I read about in paper."

The buzzer rang.

Oleg had never seen Cal so dressed up. He wore a mus-

■ 173

tard-colored leisure suit, black patent leather shoes, and a white shirt with a mustard-orange-and-brown brocade collar. Upon entering the apartment, he smiled broadly at Oleg and said to Claire, "For the lady of the house." He handed her a closed aluminum can that Oleg recognized as from the restaurant .

"Oysters!" Claire exclaimed.

"Oysters look like dead brains," Carrie said.

"Carrie, oysters are high in protein and considered very fancy," smiled Claire.

"Oysters are love food," Cal added, smiling at Oleg, Carrie, and Claire. "Sorry I'm late, by the way."

"There's still plenty to eat."

Oleg was busy serving his friend the leftover food.

"Oleg tells me you're a good cook." Every time Cal spoke, he shared a peripheral nod with Oleg. It was a habit of conspiracy learned in Mr. Perke's kitchen.

"This is the first time we've had a black person to dinner," Carrie added. "I've read a lot about black people like Harriet Tubman."

"Carrie, what's the point? We know all kinds of people. Oleg's spoken of you so often that we feel as if we know you."

Oleg and Cal stood in front of Claire's building. Dinner had been a limited success. Most of the topics of conversation had been Carrie's and included river rats, Frederick Douglass men who kill women with electric drills, and why adults lie to children. Outside, the night was dark and the moon seemed unremarkable.

"See the ring, Oleg?"

SIGNS OF DEVOTION

Oleg held his hand up to Cal's face. His eyes were filled with light. "Is it not lovely?"

"Beautiful, Oleg. You know, I'm going to one big card game tonight. I could really make a killing. I have on my new duds. You like my suit? What I need are some accessories. And you know what would make a fine accessory?" When Oleg didn't answer, Cal continued. "Your ring, Oleg. I'd give it back tomorrow."

"Is too valuable to me."

"I know, Oleg. I'll take care of it. Don't sweat."

"I cannot give away my property. Sorry, Cal, but ring is mine."

"I know it's yours, Oleg. I just want to flash it around for you. What good is it on your hand when you're fast asleep in bed?"

"Is my dream."

"Is just what my luck needs."

"I can say maybe okay but just for one night. You will write a note saying I can have backsies."

"Where do you get your English?"

"Man at pawnshop says 'backsies.'"

"You'll have the ring tomorrow. I'll give you a bonus if I do fine tonight."

"I can go to card game, Cal? You can wear my ring, but American card game is great event to me like World Series."

"You play stud?"

"No."

"Well, there's no spectating in this game. It's pretty rough."

Oleg handed Cal the ring and folded the note into his wallet. He waved good-bye.

CALIFORNIA

The first day that Cal was out of work Oleg assumed he'd had a late night playing cards. He told Mr. Perke he was certain that Cal would be back the next day. Mr. Perke didn't seem to believe him, but then again, Mr. Perke didn't believe anyone. Oleg didn't think that Cal had a phone, but he got his address from the employee punch-in card.

"Hey, Leg, stop with the oysters and get the soup crock ready," Perke called.

"Yes, I do."

"I don't care if you do or don't. Get the lousy soup in the crock."

Oleg had heard that the West Side once had great mansions. He remembered reading the descriptions in *Sister Carrie*. Here he was riding down the same street that Dreiser had described, West Jackson Boulevard. He saw a great many television repair stores and some large, mysterious warehouses. He wondered if nothing else happened on the West Side but TVs breaking down and needing treatment. He was happy that his own black-and-white set still worked. The antenna needed occasional adjusting, and he'd added a few pieces of tin foil for better reception, but that was to be expected.

Number 2121 West Jackson was a red three-flat with gray trim. When he rang the bell, a dog began barking. He wondered if it was Cal's dog. Cal had never mentioned owning a pet, not even when Carrie had asked him directly at dinner.

"What do you want?" a woman was saying.

"Is Mr. Weathers home, please. I am friend from work."

"Mr. Weathers ain't never home. Not now. Not later. Mr. Weathers don't work either. You sure you got the right person?"

"Cal Weathers. Father of three boys. Card player. Once incarcerated."

"Once plus about four. Cal will take what ain't his no matter whose it is. See my wedding ring?"

Oleg looked down at her empty hand.

"That's right. Ain't one there. Used to be, but Cal needed it back. Let's just say I wasn't too willing to give it to him. Did he take something from you too? If he did, you understand I ain't responsible. I don't know why people go around trusting that man. He seems so friendly, don't he?"

A little boy came up to the door and looked peevishly at Oleg.

"You are Baby Cal?"

The boy wrapped himself around his mother's legs. "I call him Calvin. It means something to name a child. I ain't calling this one Cal. Bad luck."

"Please, but Cal is never here?"

"Oh, he tries sometimes, but it's always the same. Too much of everything but sense."

"I am sorry to be bothering you. I loan Cal a ring, a diamond, that I buy at pawnshop. Then I don't see Cal anymore."

Oleg thought of looking behind him to see what was amusing her so.

"Would you loan a dog a steak?"

"Foolish use of good meat."

"Right," she smiled. "By the way, my name's Freddy. Short for Fredericka."

"Is nice name."

"You wanna come in?"

"Thank you, but I must go."

"Where are you from, anyway? Germany or somewhere?"

"No, I am Russian. Oleg Lum."

"Stop hanging on me, Calvin. Go watch TV. Well, if I see Cal I'll tell him you're looking. I'd call the police if I was you. No two ways about it."

Oleg took two buses directly to the Adler Planetarium, where they presented something that Carrie called a Sky Show. He sat back in his plush blue seat and looked up as a projector first showed him the sky above the Equator at Christmas and then the North Pole at Easter. Names of constellations clicked in his head like train stops. Oleg watched an eclipse of the moon darken the false sky. He wondered why writers call stars diamonds when diamonds are real.

Oleg was sleeping when the doorbell rang. He'd dozed off reading the Yellow Pages ads for adoption lawyers. Several had mentioned handling difficult cases. One ad that attracted him contained a crude line drawing of a stick figure pushing a baby carriage into which a stork was dropping a parcel. He'd call that lawyer in the morning.

He looked at the Mickey Mouse alarm clock he kept on his bedside stand. It said 3 A.M. He wandered to the buzzer in his underwear. Keeping his door chained, he cautiously looked down the hall. Soon he saw Cal walking up the stairwell wearing the same clothes he'd had on when Oleg and he had parted last. He could see the red veins in Cal's eyes and the stubble of beard decorating his prominent, poorly hinged chin.

"Where you were?" he asked Cal.

SIGNS OF DEVOTION

"I were playing cards, man," Cal mumbled. In his fatigue, he could hardly get his words out. Oleg had the impression that he was speaking from inside a locked room. "Ain't you gonna invite me in?"

Oleg unchained the door and directed Cal to sit at the end of his hide-a-bed. Oleg took the chair opposite. Feeling exposed in his underwear, he found himself crossing his legs and folding his arms in front of him.

"Practicing yoga?" Cal laughed.

"It is middle of night and I am cold."

"Sure, you was sleeping. Plus, you've given up on me already. You probably called the police."

"I do not call police but I visit Mrs. Weathers on West Jackson Boulevard."

"You visited my mother?"

"I visit a young woman named Freddy."

"Why did you want to see her?"

"I am thinking you live there. I want to see you."

"You're probably looking for this."

Oleg looked in Cal's extended hand. He was holding a ring, but it didn't appear to be Oleg's ring.

"You are magician?"

"What do you mean?"

"You change my lovely Mason ring into this!" Oleg switched on another light and rotated the ring above the bulb. "This ring is maybe glass or even worse." He returned it to Cal's hand.

"Sorry, my man, I got confused with my new wealth." Cal opened another big palm and held up Oleg's ring.

Oleg placed it on his finger. "Thank you, Cal."

"You can have the other one too. The gang banger I got

it from says it's real. Take it to your friend at the pawnshop and see. I have to go now."

"See you at work."

"No way. My winnings will last me a month if I'm careful. Perke can shove his oysters you know where." Cal reached around and telegraphed a kiss to his ass.

Oleg spent the next few minutes practicing Cal's obscene gesture. He smiled into the mirror as the ring caught the light of his movements.

SOMETHING TO ADMIRE

■ ■ ■ ■ ■ ■ ■ ■ ■ The tall Vietnamese woman held her son's hand as he circumnavigated the ice-skating rink. She half-ran, half-walked to keep up with him. Lawrence imagined that she was wearing sandals on bare feet, but he saw stylish boots, ones that a weekend hiker might order from a Lands' End catalog. His own rented skates were laced tightly, but he hesitated at the gate of the rink. Not that he didn't want to skate. It was the best way to get away from the heat of this particular summer. Even Rinny panting on the tile kitchen floor reminded him that he'd owed his dependents a better life. Rinny was the only one who'd stuck it out. Gwen and Brian were probably in Boston by now, visiting her parents and looking for a suitable apartment in Cambridge. Then she'd settle in with her usual care, choosing just the right off-white paint and subtle accessories for her new life teaching art history. He'd kept Rinny, his teaching job at the junior college, and a sadness that instructed his ankles to tremble onto the ice.

In the middle of the rink, several girls, lanky and blond like Brian but probably a little bit older, were figure skating. Occasionally the Vietnamese mother and her son would pause to observe them skating backward. She'd say something that would cause the boy's face to contort in thrilled laughter. Maybe she was promising him that come next summer, he'd skate as well as those American girls.

SOMETHING TO ADMIRE

Lawrence doubted it. The girls were able to keep their balance on one leg as they flipped over in midair. It was a natural act for them, like lighting a cigarette used to be for Lawrence. His hand gripped the rail. So far he'd done little skating, but just being in a new environment made him feel more hopeful. He hadn't skated in perhaps fifteen years, though it was one of the activities he'd promised to share with Brian when he finished his dissertation, when he had more time for fun.

"Fun's pretty low on Daddy's list of priorities," Gwen had explained. She had said it kindly to Brian, but as Lawrence wobbled across the ice, he wondered if his son would want to visit him at holiday times and in future summers. Lawrence would work at being entertaining. He'd make lists of plans, the way he used to as a child, but keep them with adult resolution. He was thinking this when the back of his left skate blade hooked the right, and he tumbled forward onto the ice with a low hiss, like air escaping a balloon. He wasn't hurt, but he wasn't sure he could get up either. There was something perilous about moving, as if it would prove him incompetent in yet another area where many people are naturals.

The woman was tireless. Her son, no more than five years old, hung on to her from time to time, but she sustained him, his ballast, his will. Lawrence imagined himself in England, trying to turn Brian into a cricket player. He wouldn't know the first thing about the sport, nor would he try to learn. He began wishing ill upon the woman. Maybe she'd trip, or the little boy, worn out with motion and effort, would cry in frustration. When the black-and-white-shirted rink guard approached to ask Lawrence if he was all right, he decided to leave. The Vietnamese woman and her son were racing in competent circles.

Everything annoyed him in summer-school class the next morning. His new khaki shorts rode up his crotch. His handwriting on the board seemed childish. The air conditioner rattled. Morton next door was doing oral drills on the past participle, and his voice filled Lawrence's classroom, deflecting off the plastic chairs, metal desks, the overlarge wall clock, and the Russian women in their housedresses, gossiping as usual, while Lawrence tried to explain the homework. He wished he could drop his own class, leave the instructor's desk vacant and never return. At the same time he was sorry that he felt this way. His students had to notice his peevishness. Maybe the lack of language between them made his emotions more available to them. Maybe they could see every inflamed nerve ending in his brain as they went over infinitives, as he asked Chanh to see him after class.

Chanh was his best writing student, an older, dignified man who'd been an art teacher in Vietnam. His writing contained the details that the others' work lacked. Chanh could describe the rice crop failing and make it sound beautiful.

"Not another boat beset by pirates," Lawrence told Chanh after class. "Was everyone's boat attacked? Didn't anyone escape without incident?" Then he began quoting from the paper, how they had run out of water, how the sea had rocked them mercilessly.

"That is what happened, Professor," Chanh explained politely. He was perhaps fifty. In America he worked in an auto-parts store and wore cheap polyester shirts, the kind

SOMETHING TO ADMIRE

Lawrence's father would wear on Memorial Day to be sporty.

"Your experience has become a cliché. Didn't anything else unusual happen to you? Or did something ordinary happen?"

"So many things, Teacher, unusual and not."

"Did your wife ever leave you?"

"I was not married."

"Did you ever take a damn vacation?"

"To Disney World with my sister."

"Well then, tell me about it. Don't forget to say it was your happiest experience. That it was worth risking your life to see this phenomenal amusement park," he added, with so much malice that he immediately felt embarrassed.

"I will tell a different story, Teacher. I will tell you about my photos. I would also like for you to see my hobby."

"Bring them to my office. I'm somewhat of a photographer myself."

"They are large. They do not transport easily. Come to my apartment some evening. My sister will cook us dinner."

Desperate for company, Lawrence agreed to visit Chanh on Friday. "I'll bring some beer," he offered in a voice that he heard straining to be jolly.

He thought he'd clean something up. He settled on the refrigerator, which was almost bare. Removing the Spicy V-8, the wilted celery, and a half-eaten tube of liver sausage, he sponged down the shelves. When he opened the freezer, which he hadn't done since Gwen and Brian left a week ago Friday, he saw the frozen slabs of meat. Maybe he'd be a vegetarian in his new life, his cleaner, simpler one. He got a green plastic garbage bag and began loading it with bricks of rump roast, pork shoulder, and frozen sirloin, "Good for B-B-Q," the label exclaimed. He'd make life as easy as possible. Maybe he'd pack up the dishes, leaving only three or four to eat from.

He didn't understand the whole year, why Gwen was gone and he was alone. He didn't understand why their dish towels were plaid. He hated plaid. Gwen hated plaid. Who had commandeered their marriage and steered it in so many false directions? Who had laid claim to their kitchen and filled it with the ugliness that finally caused Gwen to flee? He'd ignored most things. It was her own design she was leaving behind, the drab gray paint, the beige nondescript wood.

Rinny nuzzled the bag of frozen meat. Lawrence slipped on his shoes to take out the garbage. Rinny followed him to the door, where he whimpered to be let out.

"Go," Lawrence said. Rinny, who wanted to be walked, continued to whine. "I'm not in the mood," Lawrence said, shutting him outside. He heard Rinny howling on the porch.

Lawrence decided to fix something else. He'd change the oil in his Toyota. He'd put on his old cutoffs, his navy-blue Cubs shirt and wear some stupid hat. He'd take along a can of beer and his transistor radio. He'd jack up the car, lie on a beach towel, and drain the oil. He'd think of all the men he'd observed doing this over the years, discussing it later when the moment arose or not. "Changed the oil today," he'd tell someone or other later. Maybe the clerk at the Redi-Gas. "Yup," the clerk would say. "Take care of a car and it'll take care of you." Maybe he'd wax the car by hand after washing

SOMETHING TO ADMIRE

it. No ride through the automatic car wash, radio blaring something classical, "Adagio for Strings," that would make him ache for Gwen. He'd take care of things. He'd function. He'd call friends and ask them to supper. He wouldn't discard the dishes after all. He'd be needing them soon.

When he got outside, he noticed how cloudy it was. Wash a car and it rains, he thought. There was Mrs. Renchler reading on her porch. She'd probably ask about Gwen and Brian. She'd look at him with her tired, too wet eyes. He'd remember that she'd had major surgery for something serious, and act too polite. If he looked very purposeful, she'd see that he didn't want to be disturbed.

"How's it going?" she asked as soon as he slammed the town-house door behind him.

"Can't complain." He wondered why he called her Mrs. Renchler and not Donna. She was no more than seven years his senior. She seemed older, though. His generation had fought or protested the Vietnam War and refrained from joining in family life until it was too late to master it properly. Her generation, already married when he began college, knew game-show hosts by their first names and traded up for better properties whenever their husbands got raises at work. He knew Mrs. Renchler worked at something, but she didn't have a career in the sense Gwen had. He'd seen Mr. Renchler carrying cardboard boxes of what he sold. Apparently his firm wasn't among the Fortune 500. Here the Renchlers were, married perhaps twenty-five years, in a modest town house like his own.

"I bet the dog misses them," Mrs. Renchler said. "I hear him whining."

"He whined before. He has arthritis."

"Poor thing. I see you're working on the car. It must be nice to be handy."

It was so humid that Lawrence could feel sweat dripping into his eyes, making them sting. "I just thought I'd change the oil."

"Planning a trip? I know Jim always does that before vacation. We're flying this year to Ireland. Jim has family that we'll visit in Cork. Imagine that. Then we'll tour Wales, where Richard Burton was born."

Lawrence turned away and thought he'd begin. He propped the hood open. A fine rain began to fall and the trees shook. The Renchlers's mulberry tree had left a purple stain on the sidewalk between their town houses. He watched the stain thin out and spread like a watercolor sunset as the rain got heavier. He sat on his front stoop while the rain blew over his street. He wondered if it was raining in Boston or if this rain would travel east overnight.

Mrs. Renchler was shouting to him. "Aren't you going to close the hood?"

Lawrence ran to the car and slammed down the hood with explosive force.

Once inside, he realized that Rinny was still in the yard. He took off his squeaking wet shoes and opened the back door. The dog darted in before he could stop him. Rinny began shaking himself in the bedroom on a stack of linguistic texts and toward the French lace curtains. Lawrence took a beach towel and rubbed Rinny dry. "Some rain," he told Rinny, who jumped up on Gwen's side of the bed and closed his eyes.

SOMETHING TO ADMIRE

• • •

He bought a six-pack of Corona, his newly favorite beer, and drove to Chanh's address, a low-rent high-rise in Uptown near the college. The air had been cooled by the storm and a foreboding chill filled it, as if summer had prematurely surrendered to fall. In fall Brian would begin second grade at a new school, and Lawrence would be free to be anywhere he wanted. Usually he made Brian a cheese sandwich and turned on a UHF station that showed Japanese monster cartoons. They'd sit silently watching purple dragons devour whole cities until Brian's cheerful, pointy face would say good-bye and Lawrence would go back to his writing. Maybe he'd teach days now. Then he'd have his evenings free to entertain or bar hop if the mood struck him.

In front of Chanh's building on Lakeside, some children were playing in the sprinkler. Every child had black hair. They were from any country where strife had torn families apart. Haitian children were spraying Cambodian children with Chicago's purified water. Many were barefoot and small. The language spoken even in shouting was English. One little boy, an Ethiopian child of tremendous beauty, was shooting the others with a toy laser gun. "G.I. Joe," he sang out into the night.

Chanh's sister Ha had made an American dinner in honor of their guest. Tenderloin steaks nearly as big as the plates were surrounded by cottage-fried potatoes. The salad dressing came from a bottle that said "Rancher Roy," and everything was ready the moment he arrived. They sat around a card table covered with a plastic tablecloth depicting rowboats repeated on a white background. Here and there a duck could be seen in tall grass. The rowboats were empty.

SIGNS OF DEVOTION

Ha was younger than Chanh and less good-looking. She was perhaps thirty-five, but she was so thin that in profile she looked older. When Lawrence looked at her head-on, she resembled a studious child. When they were introduced, she offered him a very tough little hand and held on until he stopped shaking it. He gave Ha the beer, which she took to the efficiency kitchen. She returned with an aqua tumbler for each, beer filling it to the brim.

"Do you go to school?" Lawrence asked her.

"DeVry Institute. I specialize in electronics. I work in factory too, making transformer parts."

Chanh, who was dressed in a Hawaiian shirt covered with surfers, said, "She is the breadwinner. I am the student."

"You work too," Lawrence added.

"She makes more money." Both Ha and Chanh laughed broadly at this. American economics obviously puzzled them.

Lawrence surveyed the tiny apartment for ethnic touches. Mostly he saw used furniture—a grayish-gold velveteen couch, walnut veneer end tables and a braided blue circular rug. There was no evidence of a bedroom. Lawrence wondered where they slept. They were small enough to sleep almost anywhere. There was no evidence of Chanh's photos.

They ate quickly, without much conversation. Now and then Chanh and Ha would share a joke: that supermarkets sell fortune cookies, about the name of a street. Both found School Street, where no school existed, outrageously funny. It began to bother Lawrence that they probably carried on like this at every dinner. Of course, they'd speak Vietnamese and have their bowls of rice and cups of tea. Other

SOMETHING TO ADMIRE

than the change in menu, it mattered little that he was there. As quickly as he finished the beer, Ha silently took his plastic tumbler and refilled it. He must have finished four of the six beers before dinner had ended.

After Ha had cleared the table and they had shared dessert, lychee nuts and Rocky Road ice cream, Ha excused herself and Chanh invited Lawrence to sit on the couch.

"I will get the photos," Chanh said and walked down a dark hallway to the closet.

He came back holding a wide envelope half his height. It wasn't the fancy kind that Lawrence had seen ad execs carry on the Michigan Avenue bus. It must have been made in Vietnam of colored rice paper.

Chanh positioned himself on the floor at Lawrence's feet. He would sit there, he explained, and hold up his photos for Lawrence.

"Sometimes in America people think differently of beauty."

Then he searched through the envelope and extracted a surprisingly small photo, an 8 1/2-by-11. It was of a naked Vietnamese woman. She was not voluptuous, nor did she seem particularly interested in the camera. She appeared to be angry at something outside the camera's range. The second photo was of a girl, maybe fourteen years old, who was naked from the torso up. She was holding a piece of fruit and pretending that she was going to bite into it. Lawrence couldn't identify the fruit hidden in her hand. There was little play in her pretending.

Lawrence began to wonder whether it was Chanh's inability to relax the subjects that made for such detached and almost vicious attitudes, or whether it was life itself

SIGNS OF DEVOTION

during the war that made the women unable to open up to the camera. Of course, they weren't professional models. No one had trained them to ponder beauty or coyness or money, or whatever would have properly composed their faces. Chanh showed him a series of perhaps ten more women. The last one had very pointy breasts like triangles and hid her face in her hands.

"Lovely," Lawrence said, feeling at a loss.

"Thank you," Chanh replied, apparently satisfied. "I took those in my country. The next photos are different."

Chanh removed a series of snapshots, obviously shot with a camera of poorer quality.

"Here is water. Here is sky. That was my escape."

Lawrence took the photos in his hands. He wasn't sure that he could distinguish water from sky. Both swirled. Both were gray.

"Were you alone on the boat?"

"There were many people, but it was not a time to photograph them. We had too much trouble." He lit a cigarette and offered one to Lawrence.

"No, thanks."

"I have other photos," Chanh said, "but I did not take them. Many are of people I no longer know." He smoked silently. Lawrence felt paralyzed with drunkenness.

"Do you like the photos of women? I would sell them to you if you like them. I used to sell my photos in Vietnam."

Lawrence couldn't imagine what he'd do with one of Chanh's photos, hang it in the rec room? Chanh looked eager for him to reply. "How much do they cost?"

"For you, Teacher, twenty-five dollars. In Vietnam I make many hundreds with my photos."

SOMETHING TO ADMIRE

Lawrence guessed that Chanh was lying. No one would have wanted Chanh's nervous nudes, except perhaps a few American G.I.s with no sense.

Lawrence remembered an ugly scene he'd witnessed a few years ago on his way home from work. A middle-aged man in a green Oldsmobile, the car was the clearest image that remained of the man, had propositioned a Vietnamese student waiting for a bus at the corner of Broadway and Wilson. "How much for a suck?" the man had shouted. The girl had pretended not to hear him, but when the car circled the block again, the girl had run away. Lawrence had watched it all from a distance. It occurred to him now that he should have stood close to her.

"I'll buy one, Chanh," he said. He thought of offering to buy the entire sea-and-sky series. What a pretentious gesture it would have been to buy art that showed abstract suffering, art that was so personal. "I'll buy the first woman you showed me."

He'd keep the photo in his bedroom closet. Now and then an angry woman, angry at what the camera had never captured, would fall off the shelf when he reached in to get a shirt.

NOVEMBER

■ ■ ■ ■ ■ ■ ■ ■ ■ Drummond Nattingly had charted in musical notation the sound that rabid dogs made roaming France in the nineteenth century. The top note registered well above high C. He had also measured the hatbands of twentieth-century dictators for a symposium on brain size held in Montreal. Though Gail could have filled a calendar with Saturdays spent in tense limbo over the whereabouts of garden tools that Drummond had mislaid, she found his preoccupation with knowledge endearing. Anyone observing Drummond and Gail at parties hunched together, whispering like mutinous sailors on an ill-fated voyage, would have called their marriage a success.

Discovering the article on rabies that Drummond had contributed to a French magazine, Evan asked, "Dad, do you get paid for this?" Without reading it, Evan placed it on top of the stack of journals his father kept on the bedside table. His parents' bed was currently littered with Drummond's charts and graphs about Bangladesh. As if to verify his theory of the region as a laboratory for catastrophe, just three days ago a ferry boat loaded with 182 people had sunk in a monsoon. Two weeks prior to that, an entire village had vanished in a mud slide. Shortly before the mud slide, fire had swept through one of the few indoor markets, crowded with shoppers before a Muslim holiday. That one country could be beset by so much tragedy had to have meaning. Because he wasn't a religious man, Drummond consigned its significance to the sphere of metaphysics, his statistical domain.

Drummond spent his afternoons in the reference section of the university library using microfilm to chronicle the country's calamities. Randomly choosing three years, he calculated that 1.3 times a month, a natural disaster involving the loss of more than one hundred lives occurred. Sundays, followed by Tuesdays, were the most common times, even days rather than odd, and November was the most pernicious month. These facts once ascertained, he wrote letters to UNESCO, the Ford Foundation, The National Science Foundation and three international organizations of lesser status, requesting funds to travel and complete his research.

For the second time in sixteen years, Gail was pregnant. Even as she wondered how it could have happened again so belatedly, she spent her time marveling at how spring was transfiguring Chicago. Though the air was still cold, she drove with her car window down, sniffing the breeze off the lake. The perennials coming up in her yard had a poignancy she'd never noticed. Stray cats in alleys sang to her, and when she undressed at night, she caught herself patting her taut abdomen as she imagined it swelling.

Drummond was agreeable to having the baby, remembering how Evan's infant presence in the house had provided a startling solidity to objects. Walking Evan in his stroller, Drummond hadn't strayed once from the moment he inhabited. It seemed dangerous to travel even mentally from his baby's side. Still, he wouldn't prevail upon Gail to give birth if it weren't her choice. He was too old for naive romanticism. Besides, Gail's work was vital to her. What

SIGNS OF DEVOTION

would happen to her study of shark cartilage as an immunological resource if she interrupted it to raise a child?

Drummond accompanied Gail to her first obstetrics appointment and stroked her hand as the doctor, almost young enough to be their son, explained the risks of pregnancy at forty-four. He furrowed his brow upon discovering a certain slackness of her cervix and advised her to rest in bed if she began to spot. After their appointment, they toasted their second child at the Fondue Stube, where they used to eat on special occasions as graduate students.

"To my last glass of wine," Gail said, raising her goblet.

"To November," Drummond said, clanking his wineglass into hers.

While Gail rested, she thought that the best time to have a baby would have been April. Animals had their babies in spring. She had watched a show where little lynx cubs were born in a den in the North Woods. Her daughter, for she hoped it would be a girl, would be delivered in late November at a birthing center, a concept invented after Evan's arrival. Drummond would coach her and Evan could be present too. She closed her eyes and thought of names. Maybe Carolina, as in "Carolina dove" and "Carolina pink," phrases she'd discovered in the dictionary the night before. Evan Grant Nattingly. Carolina Dove Nattingly. Maybe just Caroline.

The phone rang three times. It was Jamie wondering where Evan was. He was supposed to meet her in front of the school. The next time it rang, Gail answered on the first ring. A woman whose accent intersected several continental boundaries said she had important news for Dr. Nattingly.

• • •

NOVEMBER

Evan Nattingly sat in Louis's car wondering how he could be friends with such a nerd. Louis's science fair experiment with hydroponic lettuce was far more annoying to Evan than anything his father had investigated. Evan spent half his life out of school in Louis's passenger seat watching him disappear into libraries and bookstores.

"Hurry up! I'm supposed to meet Jamie at three!"

Louis took a mechanical pencil from behind his ear and jotted notes on a miniature legal pad. Once Evan had his own car, he'd avoid Louis totally and stay away from home as much as possible. His parents were becoming stranger by the minute. Just last week Drummond had insisted that Evan show his band teacher the score of rabid-dog sounds. Drummond had pressed so hard that Evan finally put the damn magazine in his Eddie Bauer book bag and promised to show Mr. Dieter. Of course he hadn't, and of course his father had forgotten about his fleeting insistence that Evan betray his foolishness to the world.

Evan and Jamie had kissed each other repeatedly while working on a Spanish project, a list of items to pack for a trip to the Amazon. Jamie had taken care of the food and clothes. Evan had figured out the camping gear and contingencies. He was glad he went to a progressive school. The assignments were so unusual that they hardly seemed to be homework.

"You might try being on time now and then," Jamie snapped as she climbed into the back seat of Louis's car. She said nothing to Louis.

"Sorry," Evan said. "Louis had all this junk to buy for his science experiment, and then it looked like he was writing a letter at the steering wheel."

"I think your mom's home."

"Why do you think that?"

"I called looking for you and she answered."

"She won't mind if we stop in. She likes to know how humans live. She used to be one herself."

They sat on Evan's bed for a long time and listened to an old Moody Blues album that had been his mother's.

"Nights in White Satin . . ."

"Never reaching the end . . ."

They took turns singing the lines in falsetto. When the song ended, Evan kissed Jamie's neck. She kissed him on the ear and began unbuttoning her blouse.

"My mom's here," Evan whispered, though he hadn't heard a sound from her bedroom in an hour.

Then they heard feet padding around upstairs and a shower running. She usually showered before making dinner, which made sense to Evan considering that she touched shark tissue all day.

"She takes twenty minutes," Evan said.

Jamie took off her blouse, revealing small breasts with light brown nipples. Tiny nipples, Evan thought.

They lay down on his bed. He touched her breasts and tried putting one in his mouth. It felt too strange to him, though Jamie seemed to like it all right. She lay still under him. Then they rocked back and forth on his bed until they heard footsteps on the landing and then Gail's voice downstairs.

"Evan, are you home?"

He grabbed his T-shirt and pulled it over his head.

His mom was sitting at the kitchen table looking pale.

NOVEMBER

Even her eyes looked somehow lighter."

"Hi! Doing homework?"

"Jamie's over. We're doing homework together."

"A lady with a strange accent called. Dad must have gotten one of the grants he's requested."

She appeared to be gripping the table.

"Something wrong?"

"Just a stomachache," Gail said and flashed a smile that swallowed itself in self-consciousness.

Before he could leave for the three weeks in Bangladesh that the U.S.I.A. had arranged for him, Drummond needed shots for hepatitis, yellow fever, dengue, smallpox, and cholera. The doctor wasn't sure which one he was reacting to when he got feverish at the library and had to go to bed for the rest of the week.

"More tea, honey?" Gail asked on her way out the door to work. She was still fatigued and spotting a little, but she couldn't take a leave of absence at this important juncture in her research.

The week passed with Drummond succumbing to various fevers and making complicated travel arrangements between them. Gail worried about him as they kissed goodbye at O'Hare. After his plane took off, Gail would take Evan to a coffee bar and tell him about her pregnancy, news that had gotten lost in the shuffle of events the weeks before.

"Want to get some hot chocolate?"

"I'd like to, Mom, but I have to meet Jamie."

"You two see a lot of each other lately."

"I guess we do." Could his mother tell by his reticent

speech what they'd done in his bedroom on the days she'd been working?

"Will you be home for dinner?"

"I think Jamie's mom wants me to stay."

"Is Jamie's mom home when you go there?"

"Sometimes she isn't, but her older sister always is."

"Are you two serious?"

"Kind of," Evan said and stared out the window.

Gail hated being alone in her kitchen. She looked around for signs of family and found a half-eaten bran muffin on the counter. She spread butter on it and ate it standing up. She stared at the full briefcase of work she had taken home for the weekend, but it was hard to concentrate on anything but imagining her baby's features. The face would be round like hers, with her small nose and lips. She hoped the baby would have Drummond's intelligent gray eyes. Her own eyes were somehow less important in the world. She decided to take a bath and get to sleep. When Evan came home at 2 A.M., she didn't hear him open the door.

Saturday morning she planned to have breakfast with Evan and tell him about the baby. Why was Drummond leaving it all to her? So far, only he and the doctor knew. Her mother, her son, friends, colleagues, and the rest of the world had no idea. She remembered telling everyone the minute she and Drummond knew about Evan.

"Evan, we need to talk," she said, knocking at his door.

"What time is it?"

"Ten."

"Damn. I have a field trip to Argonne National Lab. The bus leaves in thirty minutes. Can you drive me?"

NOVEMBER

"We'll have to hurry."

Her gray cotton jogging pants barely fit over her stomach anymore. Bending over to lace her shoes, Gail felt a twinge of pain in her abdomen, followed by a wave of nausea that left her weak. She sat on the bathroom floor observing the shining wavy lines that floated over the real lines of the tile. She wished that Drummond were home. Standing up, another sharp pain gripped her. She wet a washcloth, scrubbed her face, and splashed water onto her eyes.

"What time will you be home?" she asked Evan in the car.

"Kind of late. I think I'll be at Jamie's for dinner again."

Another pain shot through her. She concentrated on keeping her foot on the gas.

"I want you home for dinner tonight. That's final."

Jamie was waiting in front of the bus. When she saw Evan, her face lit up.

Evan waved to her and bounded up the stairs without looking back at Gail.

Gail was planning on driving straight home and calling the doctor when the pains suddenly stopped. Maybe she'd sit in the park before she went home to rest. She chose a bench close to the playground. At her distance the scene was an abstract of color and good cheer. She angled her head up to the sun, closed her eyes and allowed the light to bathe her forehead, cheeks and chin.

"Excuse me" were the next words she heard.

A father and son had taken possession of a nearby bench. The pardon was meant for the son, whose ball had landed at Gail's feet.

She formed a smile that was supposed to denote understanding but meant much more to the father. He told her his name was John, that he had joint custody of Justin, worked in a Shaker furniture store, missed being married, thought Reagan was destroying civil liberties, liked to try meatless recipes and had had disk surgery two years ago. To this banquet of information, John added another fact—that he found Gail attractive.

Just as she was thinking of escaping, Justin asked her to watch him play catch with his father. For twenty minutes, she followed the ball as it passed between them. Now and then Justin looked to her for approval and she nodded in recognition. Then the pains began again, first perceived as a quickening of her heartbeat and a chill beginning at her scalp. Grimacing, she doubled over. After the pain ungripped, Gail sat up straight and looked at her watch. When the sequence repeated itself three minutes later, she knew something was terribly wrong.

"John," she shouted, and waved him toward the bench.

"I'm sorry," she began, "but I think I'm having a miscarriage. Can you get me to a hospital?"

Despite John's whispers of reassurance in the car and the doctor's lack of commitment to the worst possible scenario, she had miscarried by 4 P.M. The miscarriage itself hadn't been as bad as the cramps that preceded it. Three more sharp pains led to a gush of blood, a feeling of general weakness, and a semi-faint in which she imagined that Drummond was at her side and that Evan was being born.

Then she lay in a hospital bed with a clear tube in her arm. The doctor said that a D & C might be necessary but that she could rest for now. Assuming that John was her husband, one nurse asked if she'd like to see him. Thinking

NOVEMBER

she'd thank him for getting her to the hospital, Gail said yes. When the nurse returned, she told Gail that it seemed he couldn't be found.

She drifted to sleep and dreamed she was in her house having dinner in an empty room when she heard a sound like "Kuk! Kuk!" In flew a hummingbird, which fluttered over her plate, and then disappeared upstairs.

Waking in a panic, Gail dialed Evan.

"Mom, you sound terrible."

"I'm at St. Francis Hospital. I'm all right, honey, but you need to come here so we can talk."

"What happened?" Evan asked, his voice shivering.

"I'll tell you later, Evan, but I'm really okay."

Locating Drummond would be nearly impossible. She had the number of two hotels he'd be using but couldn't remember which one was first or what time it would be in Dacca. Waiting for Evan was unbearable. Before he knew he was going to have a brother or sister, she would have to tell him he'd lost one.

"C'mon, it's fine to feel terrible," the nurse said, observing her miserable expression. Gail acknowledged the nurse by pushing some tears into her eyes. She knew she'd cry later, when the parks were full of women who had names for their babies, small insignificant names.

When she opened her eyes again, Evan was standing over her.

"Have you been here long?"

"Just a minute. Why are you here, Mom?"

She motioned for Evan to sit. He slumped into a chair and kneaded his face with his fingers.

■ 202

"Evan, I was pregnant, but then I had a miscarriage."
He looked down at the floor. "Mom, I didn't even *know*."
"I'm sorry, honey."
"Does Dad know?"
"He knows I'm pregnant. He doesn't know I'm here."
"Are you going to tell him?"
"Of course. When we find him."
"Can I call Jamie?"
"Why?"
"I just need to tell her."

Gail watched Evan's back as he dialed the phone. She remembered how she had loved to kiss him between his perfect little shoulder blades when he was little. As she listened to Evan telling Jamie about her miscarriage, Gail felt surprised at the news.

"Jamie says she's sorry."
"We're all sorry," Gail said and reached to hug Evan.

The doctor found Drummond the next morning at the second hotel on the list. Gail was preparing to go home. Since she'd come in unexpectedly, Evan had brought clothes for her to wear. She hadn't thought of telling him what she would need. When the call from Drummond came through, she'd just discovered that Evan hadn't packed any underwear.

"Gail, I'm sorry," the scratchy voice said. For a minute they both breathed together in sympathy. Then Gail sighed. It was hard to believe in Drummond at this distance.

"Me too," she finally said.
"Shall I come home?"
"No need," she said wearily.

NOVEMBER

• • •

The cab dropped her in front of the house. She gave the driver, who'd been playing loud gospel music, her last ten dollars and went inside. She was lying on the sofa when she heard noises in Evan's room. She dragged her leaden self up the stairs and stood outside his closed door listening to the headboard banging against the wall and bicycle wheels humming. Then a girl screamed, and Gail opened the door.

"Evan!" she shouted as he dived under the covers.

"Mom!"

"How are you feeling?" Jamie asked in a voice full of composure. She had smoothed her hair and arranged Evan's Marimekko car and truck sheets so that they covered all but her neck and face.

"You have to leave," Gail said without looking at her. "Evan, get dressed and come downstairs."

Evan and Gail sat at the kitchen table. They were drinking canned mushroom soup and looking at a map of Bangladesh. Evan found Dacca on the map. Drummond's unpronounceable hotel was named after the local river. They took turns practicing its impossible name. Gail began laughing at how Evan struggled with the word. Evan was so glad to hear her laugh that he tried to hold the sound in his ears. Pressing his hands over his eyes, he thought of Jamie's hard little nipples and wondered why he suddenly hated her forever.

TWO MEN

■ ■ ■ ■ ■ ■ ■ ■ ■ If someone asked me to identify them now, I'd say that Fran was the one who followed women into washrooms, but that the man I knew better was Ted. He was more of a homebody, and sometimes I saw him on Sundays out with the whole family. They'd go for a drive or to see the dinosaur skeleton at the museum. He'd dress up on Sundays too. That was one way to tell them apart if you didn't know them well. Fran never dressed up, not even on the day in question. You'd see him in a flannel shirt, maybe some jeans or chinos, and always the same loafers. Casual was how he dressed. It describes thousands of men in a big city. That's why I wonder how the woman was able to spot Fran on the street so easily. He was average in every way but a few, which is true of most guys I know.

Ted met Fran at work, which is where I met him too. We all worked in the Chicago Park District field house on Seeley. Ted taught stuff to kids: woodshop, ice skating, whatever they needed to know. He was an expert in a minor way. He didn't know how to fix big things, but if a kid's tire needed air or there was a bookend to make, he could do it. You could say he was good with his hands. Fran didn't do much at work. I heard Ted say that being who he was made Fran think he was special, meaning his father was so damn important in the city that Fran thought he could get away with things. He'd take long lunch hours. Once, at three in

TWO MEN

the afternoon, I saw him with two women in his Mustang right in front of the field house, when he'd punched in for noon. I flashed him a little wave, a jaunty little wave, but all the time I'm thinking this guy deserves trouble, not that I wished it on him.

I used to talk a lot with Ted, sometimes about Fran. From time to time, Ted agreed with me about him. "Sure," Ted would say, "Fran has no discipline. Life has handed Fran a prize. Shouldn't he unwrap it?" I guess he was right, but there were a few things about Fran that I just couldn't swallow.

His hat, for instance. Even on the coldest day he wouldn't wear a hat, but on the hottest day of summer, there is Fran in a hat that would have made Frank Sinatra burst into song, a shiny black fedora with a little gray feather in the hatband. His feet are up on the desk. He's reading a magazine. "Can I get you anything?" I ask him.

"How about a Coke?" he says.

The other thing about Fran was Marie. Marie was good to look at, but whenever she came to visit, you knew to stay out of Fran's way. Fran liked to show us up in front of her. Usually he just left us alone, except Ted, of course, who he always ribbed, but when Marie was around, he had to show her that he really had great friends, friends he could say anything to.

She used to call me Teddy because Fran introduced me that way to her. I'm called Edward, so I won't be confused with Ted. But Fran thought it was like a joke to work with a Ted and a Teddy. It was funny because I'm bigger than Ted and older too, but what people call you outside of the home should be up to you, not to them. By the way, she always called Fran Francis.

SIGNS OF DEVOTION

"Teddy," she'd say, and I could just see her brain making her lips move that way.

"Edward," I'd tell her. It's not too hard to remember.

"Teddy, Francis tells me that you used to be real good at baseball. Do you think if I brought Jesse here you could show him how to pitch a split-fingered fastball? The kid wants to grow up to be Bruce Sutter."

"Sure," I say, "I'll teach the kid," but I've seen Jesse and know that he'll never get it right. The kid is skinny as a rail and slouches. Fran pretty much ignores him. If I had to look after that kid, I'd take him by his belt loops and show him how to stand up straight. After this big discussion, she only brought him around once for about eight minutes.

"Thanks, Teddy. Francis isn't very good at sports," she says, and then maybe she winked at me, but I really don't remember all the details.

Another thing about Francis P. Drake is his name. It's the kind of name that travels well. Not that he's real rich, but he could go places if he wanted. If I had a dad like his, head of Streets and Sanitation in the third-biggest city, I'd ask to go to France. What does a guy like me want with France? Well, I'd like to see the plane trees. Not that I'm an expert on horticulture, but I do keep things in order around the field house. On a postcard somewhere I saw these trees that look like they've had a close shave. There were a few Frenchmen playing checkers on the card too, but mostly I was interested in the background. That's the kind of guy I am. Well, I ask someone about those trees, and he tells me they just grow that way. Nobody lifts a hand. I'd like to visit a country where trees do so much on their own. Of course, there are all the museums, but mainly I'd go just to see those trees.

TWO MEN

So one day in December before Christmas Ted and I are eating lunch in the game room. They call it the game room because on Tuesday and Thursday night the seniors play bridge in there. We've ordered a pizza. It's pepperoni because that's what we always get. And the phone rings. It's Frank Baldertelli. He's a cop in the area, tall and husky as a bear. If he really had to chase a criminal, I don't doubt he'd have a few chest pains. Sometimes he comes into the field house to warm up or make a few phone calls. He calls and tells us that we'd better get down to the Clark Street Station right away. He says that someone we know is eager to see us. That's all he'll say, and he says it in such a way that if voices had mouths, his would be smirking.

We take Ted's Cutlass because he likes to keep it warmed up in winter. Even if he has nowhere to go, he'll go out and warm it up twice, maybe three times a day. We get in his car and without any introduction, like he's clairvoyant, he says, kind of muffled, "It's Fran."

"What's Fran?" I ask, looking at a street corner where a mom and her twenty kids are standing. If he'd said, "There's Fran," I would have thought he meant standing on the corner too, but he said "It's." That's different.

"Fran's in trouble again," he says.

"Was there something I missed?" I ask because I don't understand what he means when he says "again."

"No, you didn't miss a thing," Ted says and then he turns on the radio like he doesn't want to talk to me.

"Cold Sweat" by James Brown comes on, which is funny because here we are heading for a police station and James Brown is in jail too. I have to laugh at that, but I don't tell Ted what I'm laughing at. You don't have to share everything with someone just because he's driving you in his car.

And then I think that once in everyone's life, a man runs a little afoul of the law. Maybe he drinks too much and pisses on a damn tree. And just at the moment when his stream has reached midway up the trunk, a cop taps him on the shoulder and it's off to jail. Not that Fran would piss on a tree in winter. I don't doubt he'd piss on a tree, but not when the wind chill is seven below.

When we get to Clark Street, Ted says he needs to talk to me before we go in. He's real quiet and more serious than I've ever seen him. His head looks like it's sitting lower on his neck than usual, and his voice is pretty soft, like we're on a crowded bus and someone might overhear us.

"Fran has a problem," he says to me. "I know he's a grown man, Eddie, but sometimes he can't control himself."

Why's he telling me this like I'm a little boy? I wonder. "C'mon, Ted, I can take it," I feel like saying, but I just listen because he looks so sad and his sadness is clouding over the car windows.

"Fran follows women and sometimes he touches them."

That's the last thing he says. He charges out of the car and marches off with his hands in his pockets. Nothing he's done since he's gotten into the car seems to follow anything he's just finished doing. His movements and what he's told me about Fran, or hasn't told me, don't connect. The way he walks doesn't make a hell of a lot of sense either, considering how careful he usually is. That's what you can count on with Ted, that he'd walk fifty yards out of his way not to get snow on his cuffs. But now he's not even looking where he's going, which is how he ends up banging his head on a branch.

TWO MEN

"Damn," he shouts. I can hear the thud all the way back where I'm standing. He turns around to show me. His forehead is scratched pretty deep, and a big purple welt is growing under the gash. All of this trouble in four feet of walking, and we have about six yards more to the entrance. I look at my watch and wonder how long ago the cop called. It seems like about six hours.

I'm wondering what we'll see when we get inside. Will he be locked up, or what?

We walk up to the front desk and Ted says hi to lots of different officers. He's been here before, that's for sure, and maybe for the same reason.

"That's Officer Pantel," he says, pointing to this beautiful redhead with a pile of curls on her forehead. "She's married to a sergeant."

They've got Fran in a little room that looks like the principal's office in a new high school. He looks a little sick, but maybe I'm just imagining how I'd feel if it was me.

"So?" Fran asks, looking directly at Ted. "Are we ready to go?"

This confuses me a little. Has there been a crime committed or not?

"Just a minute," I say. "Don't we have to make bail or anything?"

"Eddie," Ted says, and tells me with his eyes that I'm supposed to be quiet. "I think we're ready to go."

I would have taken the cue and just shut up, but Fran has to open his big mouth.

Frank looks angry at the world for a minute. He seems to be sneering at Ted, but then his eyes pin me, and he says out of the blue, "Jesse said your fastball was for shit." He smiles at me with his smug criminal face, and I notice for the first time how crooked his teeth are.

First of all, Fran doesn't see Marie anymore, so Jesse must have told him that sometime before Christ was born. Sutter hasn't been on the damn Cubs for a century. I decide not to respond. The guy's sick anyway. Maybe he can't help how his mind spins.

"And Ted said so too," he adds.

I look at Ted, who's got a welt on his forehead the size of a pitcher's mound. It seems to be growing as I look, and Ted looks red in the face, like what Fran's saying is probably true, but he's sorry I found out. I guess the bump must be throbbing by now, so out of sympathy for Ted, I decide I'll just play stupid.

On the way out, Fran stops at the front desk, like he's checking out of a hotel, and gives that pretty redheaded cop a big hug. She hugs him back with her long, freckled arms.

So just as we're about to walk out the front door, I ask Fran what he did.

"You mean he doesn't know?" he asks Ted and looks at me like I've missed a grade in school.

By now we're in the car, and Fran adjusts the front seat so I can ride in back. I don't object. Any way you look at it, whether it's because of his special hat or his special father or his special crime, he probably deserves to sit right up front.

"I followed a woman into a john," Fran says. "That's all."

He's nonchalant because he does it all the time. And

TWO MEN

maybe when he peers over the stall, they don't notice. Or sometimes maybe they see his white sweat socks and penny loafers under the door and scream their lungs out.

"Before she went in, she was looking at me," Fran continues. "She was definitely looking at me. She's pretty young, maybe twenty. Her hair's all curly and black. It's real shiny, so she must color it. She's wearing jeans and real tall boots, mean boots. So I finish getting my prescription. That's why I was there in the first place. That gives her a minute to go into a john and choose a stall. That's the way it is in the ladies' room. Whatever women want, they get a private booth.

"I hesitate a moment, then I open the door. She's not in a stall after all, and she probably doesn't think I'm a janitor because—for one, I don't look like a janitor, plus I didn't knock, like a male employee would. But since she looked at me already, she must know I've come for a reason.

"She's fixing her makeup in the mirror. She has a wand out and is doing her eyes. She watches me watching her in the mirror. She has a good face, but it's not terrific. I guess she'd be pretty plain without a paint job. She doesn't say anything, and I don't either.

"She just keeps doing the makeup. Back and forth across her eyelids, like a kid drawing some sky. Now she's adding mascara. She puts some on her top lashes, and then with her tongue out to help her concentrate, she paints the bottom lashes. The tongue looks awful sexy.

"I decide I'll come around behind her. I'm close enough to smell her hair spray, her deodorant. I'm reaching out to kiss her neck. She whirls around and pokes the mascara toward my eye. It gets me in the cheek instead. There's a dark-blue smudge on my right cheek. Then the bitch runs out of the bathroom. I spend a long time using toilet paper to get the mascara off of my face.

"I don't see her when I leave the john, but before I make it back to my car, there she is sitting in a cop car pointing at me, and her mouth's waving like a flag."

So now we're back at the field house and I see these two men in a new way. Fran is sick, it's as simple as that, and Ted is probably his only friend in the world.

And where do I fit in this little equation? I wonder as I blow snow off the sidewalk that afternoon. The sky is gray, and by the time I've finished the path to the parking lot, snow has covered up the sidewalk again.

Knowing what I do about Fran, I guess I'm more like Ted. And knowing what I do will just give me more responsibility around the field house, making sure he doesn't do anything unseemly during work hours. That's the first thing I think.

More than that, though, I think that both of us, me and Ted, would be better off in France without Fran. For one, I'd get to see those plane trees, and if Ted wasn't looking where he was going for once in his life, it wouldn't be a problem like it is here in America.

AS SURE AS ALBERT SCHWEITZER

"You're not my friend," I hear myself saying, and regret it already.

"Of course not. I'm your sister," Ariel assures me, and both are true.

We've been sisters for forty years, assuming that sisterhood begins at birth, and not friends for almost as long. A photo of my babyhood is entitled "pain" in my memory bank, my toe turning purple between Ariel's clamped teeth, my lips rounding into a perfect little scream after my father captured the eerily lit image. In truth, our sisterly connection had begun earlier, when she requested me like a mail-order bride. "A gleam in my sister's eye" is how I think of myself. Knowing her formidable nature, my parents produced me in ten months.

It would have been nice if we'd been close, like the Fuller girls down the street. They were identical twins, the type that plot arson in secret code. Later they moved to the Left Bank and embraced Marxism doubly and passionately. I can see them spouting party line in unison, two heads bobbing above identical black trench coats. Once when we played with the Fullers, they attacked us after exchanging menacing stage whispers. I sustained five bites. Ariel ran home and didn't tell Mom about the carnage down the street.

AS SURE AS ALBERT SCHWEITZER

Ever since Ariel divorced Steady Fred (that's what the whole family called him) and married Walter, we've been less friends than before. The problem with Walter is that you want to spill gravy on his tie when he's not even wearing one. Walter eats as if he's proud of the way he handles a fork. He gives Ariel practical presents, like the world's smallest folding umbrella, and Ariel gushes. They met at her baseline mammogram, which is Walter's medical specialty. Poor Fred is a novelist who's devoted himself to translating from the Chinese since Ariel cast him off two Christmas Eves ago at my house in front of the entire family. He says his translations will promote world peace, his new goal. He's joined the Nuclear Winter Protection Society, the Ozone Layer Watch, the Strontium Ninety Measurement League, the Fathers for Safe Soil, and the Free Joseph Rhinestellar Coalition since Ariel said good-bye. He talks with passion about Joseph R., a Lithuanian ax-murderer, whose crimes were political and justly motivated.

Today Ariel has come over for lunch. It's a tactic we try every few months. Our Reykjavik, I call it, and carefully choose what to serve because Ariel sees meanings everywhere.

"That salsa's too red," she says. "Who do you think you're fooling?"

"I bought it at the Mexican grocer."

"If I were you," she says, "I'd shop Costa Rican. Costa Rica's a neutral nation. You can trust them."

"Is that supposed to be a joke?" I ask. Maybe everything she says is a joke, but I've missed the punch line for forty years.

"And I'd buy free-range chickens. I bet this one got plump on steroids."

"She was a bench-press champ before she met her tragic end."

Ariel laughs too hard. Sometimes instead of laughing, she plain out sneers, so her laughter is perplexing. Why should I have to serve an annotated lunch, and should I tell her I'm trying to get pregnant after all these years? Whenever I announce normal events to her, she greets them with suspicion. She'll probably ask me whose baby it will be, as if I haven't been married to Jonas forever.

"I'm thinking of leaving Walter," she offers.

"That's surprising, Ariel," I say, too enthusiastically.

"He's a real snooze. Why did I get caught up in his act, which includes a real problem with women?"

"I never suspected."

"He'll listen to me forever," she sighs, pensive, morose. "I can't stand to hear myself talk anymore. Everything I say he takes so seriously. He burst into tears when I told him about a problem at work. 'Oh, it's so hard to be a woman!' he said, as if he would know. 'I'm so sorry for you,'" she says in a cloying baritone.

"Too much Alan Alda," I say.

"I happen to like Alan Alda."

"Too much Leo Buscaglia," I try.

"Who do you like?" Ariel asks, offended.

"Too much Pope John Paul," I offer.

"Have you no shame?"

Ariel is as devout a Catholic as a divorced woman married to a Jew can be.

AS SURE AS ALBERT SCHWEITZER

Now I unveil the dessert, which will soon be a postmortem under her microscope.

"That's beautiful," she says of my fruit tray. "Did you make it yourself?"

"In the sense of arranging it, yes. In the sense of having godlike powers, no."

The phone rings. It's Walter. Judging from Ariel's tender phone voice, he hasn't been informed yet.

"He wants to go away for the weekend. I have to go shopping and then pack, Charlotte."

"But you hate him, and we were going to talk about Mom and Dad. We were going to plan for their future. We were going to solve the world food shortage. We were going to end war and leave the world a little more intelligent than when we were hatched."

"I think you have us confused with the Fuller twins."

Later that week, I'm to have my baseline mammogram. It's a ritual of turning forty. I hear it's a new form of torture that makes one forget the mental anguish attendant to that anniversary. Your breasts are squeezed into a vise for vertical and horizontal views. *Click Click.* "Because it's good for you," you keep thinking as you picture liver and peas on a plate and the vise is withdrawn.

An hour after Ariel leaves, the phone rings. It's Walter again though I was hoping for Jonas, who knows how to laugh, seven on a scale of six.

"When did Ariel leave?"

"Long ago, Walter."

"She doesn't love me anymore."

"How do you know that?"

"She never comes home."

"Where does she live, the park?"

"She sleeps here, but she lives at the movies. She'll see anything, even war movies."

"Funny, we never discuss movies."

"It's her secret life."

"Like an affair."

"Like an infatuation with anyplace but here, so I decided we'd fly to Cannes this week for the Festival. If it's movies she wants, I'll give her movies."

"A VCR would be cheaper."

"I hate small screens. They remind me too much of my work."

We say good-bye because I have to visit Mom and Dad this afternoon. One of the worst indignities of life is that it is too stupid and slow for some people. That's true of my parents, who cohabit a double room with sunset-orange bedspreads at the Magnolia Tree Retirement Home. My father calls it the Mongolian Tired-of-It-Home. The plans that Ariel always avoids making involve a burial fund. It's not that we want to think of their deaths, but Mom, the frustrated Chief Executive, wants everything in waiting. I already know what dress she'll wear. It's a simple navy sheath, perfect for the seed pearls she keeps in a special purse for the occasion.

"Your father's not here today," she says. She can't see very well and has taken to wearing dark glasses and a visor. She looks like a poker dealer on a Golden Age cruise. Her one affectation is to have her hair done by the beautician who comes weekly. Andrei is a master of the French roll, which my mother has worn since her fiftieth birthday. It's gone

AS SURE AS ALBERT SCHWEITZER

from auburn to honey blond to stark white with a tropical-pink cast in sunlight. The rest of her has faded and shrunk. If she were a painting, I'd have her restored. Since she is my mother, all I'm able to do is listen with all my attention twice a week.

"Where is Dad? At the track again?" Once a month Magnolia rents a schoolbus to take its inveterate gamblers to the harness races. Three weeks ago Dad won $720 on a horse named Wax.

"Why did you bet on him?" I'd asked.

"My friend's nickname was Max. You know, like Max Baer. Like Groucho."

"But that's Marx."

"Marx, Max, what's the difference? There's this horse Wax, but I misread his name, Max. Three minutes later I have two dollars to the nth power."

Mom pours me some tea that she's warmed on the hot plate and hands me a huge jar of honey. "Dad's having some X rays today," Mom explains nonchalantly. "The doctor thinks there's something wrong with a kidney or two."

"Is it serious?"

"At our age everything, including breakfast, is serious."

"Which reminds me," I tell her, "Ariel won't be taking you to breakfast Sunday. She's going to France with Walter."

"Lousy tit doctor."

Mom's still attached to Fred, who possibly liked her more than he liked Ariel.

"Walter's good for her, Mom. Freddy didn't care if she was dead or alive, as long as she was quiet."

"Quiet is something we all need, dear. Mrs. Frye next

door could have quiet explained to her a few thousand times. I've never known anyone so dead set against quiet."

"She has bad nights, Mom."

"She could put a pillow over her head."

"You could close your door."

Mom looks sad. Her mind wanders and sometimes I wonder where it's gone. At other times she looks ecstatic, like a college sophomore who's just discovered Sartre.

"I was just thinking about Frank Sinatra," she says. "Once I saw him sing in Las Vegas, and I thought if I could have met him, my life would have been different."

"A life can really swerve, I guess. Like the day Dad bet on Wax."

"I'm not talking about chump change. I'm talking about love. One minute you're young, and Frank Sinatra is skinny and hopeful. The next minute you're old and he is too."

"So what would you have done if you'd met Frank Sinatra?"

"I'd have had an affair. I'd have talked to him in bed. Maybe it would have helped. He got so harsh later in life, like he was disappointed by something."

"How could you tell that?"

"I saw him on Bob Hope. I read books."

"Do you think Dad will be okay?"

"Dad hasn't been okay since the transistor was invented and found a way into radios and into his waiting ear. He's like Sinatra. A real disappointment."

Dad talks about Mom in this way too. If he were here, she'd be glumly sitting in the corner while he complained about her lack of hospitality to the other residents. A few weeks ago he said, "Mom won't put her teeth in to say hello

AS SURE AS ALBERT SCHWEITZER

to Mrs. Smyrnz, who was so nice to me when Mom was sick."

"She's a manhunter," Mom called from her corner outpost. "She may not look like anything, but she's after him just as sure as Albert Schweitzer."

"I've never heard that phrase, Mom."

"Because I just made it up. It's one thing I still have full control of, language."